CC

Women Writers

General Editors: *Eva Figes* and *Adele King*

Published titles:

Margaret Atwood, Barbara Hill Rigney
Anne Brontë, Elizabeth Langland
Charlotte Brontë, Pauline Nestor
Emily Brontë, Lyn Pykett
Fanny Burney, Judy Simons
Willa Cather, Susie Thomas
Colette, Diana Holmes
Emily Dickinson, Joan Kirkby
Sylvia Plath, Susan Bassnett
Christina Stead, Diana Brydon
Eudora Welty, Louise Westling
Edith Wharton, Katherine Joslin
Women in Romanticism, Meena Alexander

Forthcoming

Jane Austen, Meenakshi Mukherjee
Elizabeth Barrett Browning, Marjorie Stone
Elizabeth Bowen, Phyllis Lassner
Ivy Compton Burnett, Kathy Gentile
George Eliot, Kristin Brady
Mrs Gaskell, Jane Spencer
Katherine Mansfield, Diane DeBell
Christina Rossetti, Linda Marshall
Jean Rhys, Carol Rumens
Muriel Spark, Judith Sproxton
Gertrude Stein, Jane Bowers
Virginia Woolf, Clare Hanson

Further titles are in preparation

Contents

Editors' Preface

The study of women's writing has been long neglected by a male critical establishment both in academic circles and beyond. As a result, many women writers have either been unfairly neglected or have been marginalised in some way, so that their true influence and importance has been ignored. Other women writers have been accepted by male critics and academics, but on terms which seem, to many women readers of this generation, to be false or simplistic. In the past the internal conflicts involved in being a woman in a male-dominated society have been largely ignored by readers of both sexes, and this has affected our reading of women's work. The time has come for a serious reassessment of women's writing in the light of what we understand today.

This series is designed to help in that reassessment.

All the books are written by women because we believe that men's understanding of feminist critique is only, at best, partial. And besides, men have held the floor quite long enough.

EVA FIGES
ADELE KING

Acknowledgements

I am grateful for the semester's study leave granted to me by Wolverhampton Polytechnic, without which this book could not have been written. I would like to thank Margaret Callender and Penny Welch for having read and discussed parts of the work in progress, and to thank my mother, Marie Holmes, for being a lucid but always encouraging first reader.

In memory of Mary
1949–1989

For hadn't niggardly love wanted to fill my cupped hands one last time with a little shrivelled treasure? In future I shall gather nothing except by armfuls. Great armfuls of wind, of coloured atoms, of generous emptiness that I shall dump proudly on the threshing floor.

Colette
Break of Day

1 The Hidden Woman: An Introduction

A man dressed in a hooded domino watches the dancers at a masked ball, not daring to remove his cumbersome disguise because he has lied in order to attend the ball alone. He recalls the conversation with his wife the night before. As a doctor he has been able to pretext an urgent visit to a sick patient to explain his inability to accompany Irene to the Opera Ball, and she has refused, with fastidious horror, the idea of going without him.

As he thinks of his gentle wife, "this trembling hind", the sound of a little cough that resembles hers draws his attention to a Pierrot, in purple and silver costume and lacy mask, perched close to him on a balustrade. The inelegance with which the Pierrot scratches its thigh relieves the husband of any suspicion that this could be Irene, but the figure produces from its pocket an antique snuff box containing a lipstick, the very box he gave to Irene for her last birthday. Shocked and distraught, the man takes refuge in "an active and normal jealousy" and follows his wife in order to discover the identity of his rival. But Irene makes her way slowly, without apparent purpose, amongst the dancers. She stops to drink champagne, invites the advances of an "almost naked wrestler", dances briefly with a warrior and kisses a young man who is reposing, out of breath, on a banquette.

Gradually the husband realises that there is no rival, no secret *rendez-vous* that would restore the situation to the safe dimensions of a mere infidelity. There is only a free, solitary and shameless Irene whom he has never known and whom "a little mask and a hermetic costume had restored to her irremediable solitude and her immodest innocence" (*CSC*, 238).

"The Hidden Woman" ("La Femme Cachée") was the title story of a volume of short narrative texts published in 1924, during a decade that saw the appearance of many of Colette's finest and best-known works: *Chéri* in 1920, *La Maison de Claudine* (*My Mother's House*) in 1922, *Le Blé en herbe* (*Ripening Seed*) in 1923, *La Fin de Chéri* (*The Last of Chéri*) in 1926, *La Naissance du jour* (*Break of Day*) in 1928, *Sido* in 1929. In several ways, and not least in the title itself, the story encapsulates essential features of Colette's writing, both formal and thematic. The setting, an elaborately theatrical Parisian soirée which brings together revellers of different social backgrounds behind the liberating anonymity of disguise, represents well the milieu of most of Colette's fiction, where a Bohemian sub-class of entertainers and kept women adjoin and at times converge with a more conventionally employed bourgeoisie.

The location of the narratives in this non-intellectual, apparently frivolous milieu, together with the focus on personal, sexual relationships led the major French literary historians and critics to refuse Colette the status of a fully serious writer and to present her as talented, but ultimately trivial. She might have been "one of the great stylists of the age" (Gustave Lanson's 1951 *History of French Literature*) but in her work "love is the great, the only theme" and Colette fails to "moralise on man and his destiny" remaining merely "on the level of natural instincts" (P.E. Charvet's 1967 *Literary History of France*), "her world . . . one of boudoirs and bedrooms" (Henri Peyre in his 1961 article "Contemporary Feminine Literature in France", Yale French Studies, 27). This lofty disparagement of what were seen as intrinsically feminine concerns typifies the gender bias of much conventional criticism and explains why the popular perception of Colette in France and possibly in England too, remains that of a writer of charming animal tales and rather spicy fiction. There is a nice irony in the fact that feminist re-reading reveals in Colette's work a radical critique of those very assumptions about gender that determined the trivialisation of her work.

The story "The Hidden Woman" also exemplifies one of Colette's recurring narrative patterns, a pattern of disruption and separation in which a couple gradually diverge until they become two separate units. In "The Hidden Woman" as in many of Colette's fictions, it is the female protagonist who moves away towards a provisional, imperfect but real form of freedom, leaving her partner bereft of a masculine identity that depended on her playing a reciprocal role. In *The Vagabond* (La Vagabonde, 1911) Renée in a literal sense moves away from Max, as she leaves Paris to travel south on a music-hall tour, a departure that prefigures her choice of "vagabondage" rather than relationship. The structure of *Chéri* provides a variation in that Chéri himself closes the narrative by leaving Léa, but if *Chéri* and *The Last of Chéri* are read as a single plot then the same structure can be perceived, for Léa moves away from Chéri into a self-absorbed old age, and this movement is echoed by Edmée's emancipation from the docile wife of the first book to the efficient, self-contained young woman of the second.

Alice in *Duo* (1934) first breaks the rules of the couple by desiring another man, then withdraws emotionally and physically from the jealous Michel, and Fanny of *The Other One* (*La Seconde* 1929), shifts loyalty from her husband to that emblem of threat to the couple, the Other Woman. Even in *Ripening Seed*, in one sense an account of the formation of a conventional couple, the basis of the relationship is seriously disturbed at the novel's conclusion by Vinca's failure to acknowledge shame or awe at her first experience of sex, and Phil's resulting uncertainty about his masculine role as he ponders "his own insignificance, his downfall, his kindliness" (*RS*, 122).

For Colette's work is frequently concerned with masculinity and femininity seen, in the full theatrical sense of the word, as roles. "The Hidden Woman" evokes the most conventional of gender roles by employing the "flashback" to present the doctor and Irene performing for each other the parts of Husband and Wife, he the preoccupied breadwinner obliged to forego pleasures for work ("And I was looking forward to this ball like a kid"), protective and solicitous ("You know you can go without me, darling"), she delicate in her white dress, beautiful in a fragile, consumable way ("her narrow face pink, matte and long, like a thin sugared almond") and too vulnerable to face a crowd alone ("Oh, no! Can you see me in a crowd, all those hands . . ." [*CSC*, 235]). In the text that follows the anonymity of disguise releases a female identity so different, so radically opposed to the Irene the husband believes he knows, that conventional femininity becomes paradoxically the disguise, and Irene's "native brutality" and natural "immodest innocence" are restored to her by the wearing of a mask.

The same theme appears in *Gigi* (1944), where the process of becoming a woman is represented as a carefully learnt concealment of the self behind a mask of "femininity", and in *Chéri* where Léa relinquishes her role in old age with a mixture of regret and relief. So too Renée of *The Vagabond* experiences the transition from the role of wife to the more explicit disguise of costumed mime as a form of liberation. On the other hand male fancy dress is identified with constraint and discomfort as Irene's husband is "embarrassed by his domino" and trips over his skirts, implying that the masculine role itself offers a degree of freedom and privilege.

The release from disguise through disguise is an apparent

contradiction, a form of the paradox which is another recurring element of Colette's writing. "The Hidden Woman" is constructed around a series of paradoxical linkages which bring together what are culturally defined as opposites. They begin with the husband's initial state of simultaneous "malaise" and "pleasure", include the multiple cases of cross-gendering, where the conventional signifiers of one gender are attributed to the other, so that a young man sits fanning himself on the edge of the dance floor and a casually dominant woman kisses his mouth "like a crushed grape", and then culminate in the oxymoron of Irene's "immodest innocence".

Both at the level of style and at the broader level of characterisation and plot, Colette's texts make unexpected associations, reverse familiar patterns, disturb neat binary division. Her best-known love story is that of a middle-aged woman and a very beautiful young man, and the tragedy is not that of the aging mistress but that of Chéri who has as we say, his life before him. Love in Colette's world is "not a sentiment worthy of respect" (*BD*, 22) but desire generally is. Jealousy, as here, may become a relief from anxiety, betrayal be "hoped for".

The narrative perspective in "The Hidden Woman" is an essential part of the meaning. The narrator is "extradiegetic" that is, external to the fiction rather than herself a fictional character, but as in several of her novels (notably *The Last of Chéri*, *Ripening Seed*, *The Cat* (*La Chatte*, 1933), despite the central concern with female identity Colette partially adopts the perspective of the male protagonist. The narrator oscillates between focalising events through the husband ("He had been looking at the swirl of masks in front of him for a long time" [*CSC*, 235] or "he thought about this trembling hind" [236]) and external focalisation which establishes a distance between narrator and protagonist ("tripping over [his domino] like a man in skirts" [235], "the man in the purple cowl" [237]). Thus whilst we are aware of a controlling consciousness not identifiable with that of the protagonist, we do perceive Irene from the husband's point of view, which means, at first, a very conventional vision of "my wife". However, Irene begins to escape definition, both by physically moving away and evading the husband's glance, and by a series of acts which can not be read within his interpretation of what constitutes "my wife".

The reader is increasingly detached from the consciousness of the husband, until finally his vision fades completely as he "disappear(s) into the crowd" and disappears syntactically. The last words to refer to him are those of the opening main clause of the last sentence "He was sure that she was not waiting or looking for anyone," but the subordinate clauses with Irene as subject then take over and sweep to the stories conclusion. Irene ends the story as subject, unmediated by her husband's perception.

This narrative technique, with its significant switches between external and internal focalisation, is the mode in which most of the novels and the short stories are written. However, Colette also makes use of a first person "intradiegetic" narrator, that is a narrator who is also a character within the fiction, who both enacts and tells the story. This is the narrative mode of the early Claudine novels and of *The Vagabond* and its sequel *The Captive* (*L'Entrave*, 1913), all of which adopt a diary form, but it is also in a slightly different way, the technique used in many of the "novellas" or "long short stories" like "Bella Vista", "The Tender Shoot" ("Le Tendron", 1943), "The Képi", in the autobiographical texts such as *My Mother's House* (*La Maison de Claudine*, 1922), and in those texts which mingle fiction, autobiography and reflection in an original fusion of genres, such as *Break of Day* or *The Evening Star* (*L'Etoile vesper*, 1946). Colette's tendency to ignore frontiers, to fuse and mingle discrete categories, is again apparent here for the narrator of stories which display all the marks of narrative fiction shares name and circumstances with the narrator of texts apparently autobiographical, and with the historical Colette. It seems useful here to adopt the strategy of Elaine Marks in her book on Colette and to maintain the important distinction between author and narrator of the text by placing inverted commas around the narrator and referring to her as "Colette".

"The Hidden Woman" is a vibrant, expertly crafted story that focuses on the relationships between gender and identity and on those between love and freedom, concluding on a note of glorious paradox. It provides an appropriate introduction to Colette's work.

2 Creative Contradictions

> You can't imagine what a queen of the earth I was when I was twelve years old. Solid, rough-voiced, with two tightly woven plaits that whistled round me like whiplashes . . . (*Les Vrilles de la Vigne*, 204)

> My childish pride and imagination saw our house as the central point of a Mariner's Chart of gardens, winds and rays of light, no section of which lay quite beyond my mother's influence . . . (*Sido*, 148)

Looking back, Colette perceived her childhood as a time of great happiness that radiated out from the safe centre of her mother's love to make the world beyond both secure and desirable. In her early fiction and in autobiographical texts rhapsodic images of girlhood contrast with the compromises and constraints of the adult woman, and since in Colette's own life a happy rural childhood ended with marriage to the faithless Willy and an attendant move to Paris, it is not surprising that critics and biographers should have viewed this transition as crucial to the writer's life and work. The dominant version of Colette's life opposes childhood innocence to adult betrayals, a lost paradise to harsh reality, the pastoral world of a country childhood to the cultural, man-made world of the city.

Colette was born on 28 January 1873 in the village of Saint-Sauveur-en-Puisaye, Burgundy and was christened

Sidonie Gabrielle. Colette was in fact her family name, a patronymic later transformed into a first name by her husband. She was the fourth and final child of Sidonie Colette (née Landoy), and the second child of her mother's second marriage. Her father was Jules Colette, once a captain in the French Army but now, having lost a leg in battle in 1856, a civil servant and Saint-Sauveur's official Collector of Taxes. The household into which Sidonie Gabrielle was born was a comfortable and a moderately affluent one: the house and several other properties besides had belonged to her mother's wealthy but dissolute first husband till his death in 1865. It was also, on the evidence of Colette's own evocation of this period, a happy household inhabited by parents who loved each other with passion but also with a sense of humour, by children of whom at least the three youngest thrived on the freedom allowed them, and by a large contingent of domestic animals.

This period ended partially when Captain Colette's inept management of the family finances led to the enforced sale of house and property in 1890 when Colette was seventeen, and the family moved to Chatillon-sur-Loing where the eldest son Achille, was now practising as a doctor. It ended finally when, at the age of twenty, Colette married Henri Gauthier-Villars, better known as Willy, and left the family home for her husband's cramped flat in Paris, his frenetic lifestyle and his infidelities.

The relevance of the "Paradise Lost" model is clear, and from a feminist perspective Colette's life provides a sort of exemplary narrative of girlhood freedom, marital oppression and the hard struggle to regain autonomy. However, what this model tends to oversimplify is the nature of childhood experience, which is not merely instinctual and emotional but also social and cultural. In late nineteenth century France, village life was already thoroughly penetrated with the dominant national culture, and this makes the genesis of Colette's radicalism as a writer both problematic and interesting. It is the plausible contention of some feminist theorists that since, in a patriarchal society, the only available discourse is a male discourse and "the world is man's word",[1] women under patriarchy are silenced or driven to the madness of non-sense. Yet Colette grew up and was educated under a deeply conservative and patriarchal regime, and produced texts which are the very reverse of silence and more lucid than mad, particularly on the politics of gender. This implies the presence in her childhood not simply of an idyllic ignorance of the social world, but of conflicts or contradictions that opened the space for question and challenge.

In some senses life in a small country town in Burgundy would have changed little for centuries: the awareness of the rhythm of the seasons, of the significance of changes in weather, of the varieties of fruits and flowers, are features of Colette's writing that emerge from an early familiarity with a relatively timeless culture. But by the late nineteenth century the isolation of the countryside was coming to an end: greater social mobility resulted from an increasing need for an urban workforce and from the rapid improvement of communications. These were the early years of the French Third Republic, and of radical developments in the provision of State education.

Anxious to strengthen the new Republic against external enemies – in particular Germany whose defeat of France in 1870 had led to the demise of the Second Empire – and against the internal enemies of an anti-Republican Catholic Church and a powerful monarchist opposition, the Republic's leaders opted to develop a sense of national identity and a more highly skilled workforce by extending and reforming State education. A series of reforms in the 1870s were followed in 1882 by a law that made education free and compulsory for all French citizens between the ages of six and thirteen. Thus, in the person of the "instituteur" or State primary school teacher and through the nationally uniform textbooks, the dominant ideology of secular, patriotic rationalism could penetrate the consciousness of the majority of the nation's children.

The provision of primary education extended to both sexes, and a law had also been passed in 1880 which established State secondary education for girls. In a regime that excluded women from "universal" suffrage, denied them legal control of their own income and of their children, and paid them on average half as much as an equivalent male worker, this is at first surprising. The reasons may have lain partly in an awareness of the changing needs of a more industrialised economy, but they were also directly ideological and articulated as such in parliamentary debates. Far from being feminist, the defenders of women's right to education were concerned with the ideological climate in which male citizens of France were formed: hitherto the major role played by female religious orders in women's education had meant that a majority of women – and particularly of bourgeois women – were practising Catholics and often opposed to the secular Republic. They were thus failing to bring up their sons in the true faith of progressive rationalism. As Jules Ferry, later Minister of Education, had stated in 1870 "There is a choice to be made, citizens. Women must belong to science or they will belong to the Church."[2] The historian Bonnie Smith sums up the argument neatly: ". . . the retrograde conditions of women's minds suddenly appeared a luxury France could no longer afford".[3]

The new school built in Saint-Sauveur in 1880 thus had a girls' section alongside the boys'. As the youngest child of an educated and moderately affluent family it would have been considered more normal for Sidonie Gabrielle to attend a convent boarding school in a neighbouring town, as her elder sister had. However, the family finances were already in a decline that was to end in bankruptcy and Sido, Colette's mother, was unwilling to part with her youngest daughter. In the village school, largely attended by "the daughters of grocers, farmers, policemen and labourers" (*CS*, 10) the child followed the same syllabus as the majority of her contemporaries.

Explicitly and unashamedly ideological, the syllabus communicated a consistent message in all areas of study, from the history and geography of France and civic morality, to grammar and practical maths. Patriotism, Republican democracy, hard work and family life were good; enemies of France, Catholicism and monarchism, dissatisfaction with one's status in life were bad. The Third Republic prided itself on being democratic and progressive, and the principles of liberty, equality and fraternity were central to the positive image of the French nation. They were, of course, very selectively interpreted, for the hegemony of a male middle class made the Republic and its educators blind to differences of class and gender, as well as to those of race when it came to colonialism. The awkward contradiction between the ideal of national freedom and the reality of imperialism was neatly resolved by maxims: "The people of the world love France, because France loves them and serves them."[4] People who failed to rejoice in the privileges of the great were characterised as lazy and envious:

> . . . it is always the idle, the good-for-nothings, who insist on attacking our great men; lazy men are invariably embittered, discontented, meanly envious and often evil.[5]

preached Payot in his widely used "Course in Morals", and the duty of male citizens to fight for France against other nations was axiomatic and used merely to demonstrate the grammatical function of the direct object: "The soldier defends his country. What does the soldier defend? His country." The school books produced at this period collectively construct a vision of French society as a happy family united against its enemies, benevolently extending the benefits of its advanced civilisation to less able and energetic races across the seas, distributing power, privilege and property unevenly but fairly on the basis of merit and responsibility.

Following a syllabus identical to that of the boys next door, but for the replacement of military drill with needlework, girl pupils were also absorbing a very coherent subtext on gender. This meant learning their own systematic exclusion from the public world and their supportive and dependent role as members of what Simone de Beauvoir some seventy years on, was to term the "second sex". This extract from advice given to women primary school teachers in 1883 demonstrates the point:

> Though the female primary school teacher can not teach her pupils military drill, she should be teaching them why their brothers undertake such exercises. She must inspire in them . . . respect for true bravery. . . . Ladies, you must teach our daughters to appreciate courage and to despise cowardice! What we ask of you is that you form – in the full sense of the word – female citizens, Frenchwomen who hold civic virtues in high esteem and whose hearts throb when they behold nobility of feeling . . .[6]

What is at issue here is not the emphasis on male warrior virtues, though that is also a significant aspect of Third Republican discourse, but the accentuation of the passive, observer status of the female. Throughout the textbooks and the publications for teachers produced at this time the French citizen is assumed to be male, and the absence of women from power is inscribed in the consistent use of the male grammatical form ("*le* Français", "our great *men*"). Women, as in the example above, appear as supportive sisters, wives or mothers of the central male protagonist.

Alternatively, they are idealised and abstracted to become the country itself, for France is consistently represented as the great mother, and thus identified with women: "Beloved France, we are your children, and all our lives we want to remain worthy of you" cry the two boy heroes of the Third Republic's most famous and longest running textbook *Two Children's Tour of France*.[7] The same message is conveyed incidentally with an air of uncontentious reference to a known reality, in the grammar syllabus, which uses as examples of the direct object: "The child loves *his mother*. The soldier defends *his country*."[8] In French the native country, or fatherland (*la patrie*) is also feminine in gender. There is nothing arbitrary here about the placing of the male nominative and the female accusative: women become the object of men's respect, veneration, gratitude, filial love, rather than the subject of their own acts or feelings. And through the identification of the native land with the mother, women are also appropriated in the service of a deeply conservative doctrine of militarism and unquestioning obedience to the State. It is perhaps not surprising that so many male novelists of the Third Republic, from the communist Nizan to the right-wing Montherlant and the fascist Drieu la Rochelle, should later have used female characters to represent the conservatism of French society.

There is a considerable gap here between the textbooks' erasure of women from the role of subject and the irreverent assertiveness which Colette consistently associates with her own girlhood, and which she makes a central feature of the schoolgirl characters in *Claudine at School* (*Claudine à l'école*, 1900) and *Claudine in Paris* (*Claudine à Paris*, 1901). In these early novels, with their strong element of autobiographical reference, Colette depicts the village school as a site of pleasure and relative freedom for the girl pupils: they are exhorted by teachers and texts to behave with decorum, to conform to the polite fiction that girls are asexual, but their response is on the whole both humorous and lucid. A much used textbook of the period, *The Good Country Housewife: simple notions of domestic economy for use in girls' schools* by one L.E. Berillon is the target of one bout of characteristic mirth:

> Oh! Berillon, how you amused those wicked girls, of whom I myself was one! Marie Belhomme, a guileless soul, would lift her midwife's hand to heaven as, her voice throbbing with tender conviction, she mockingly apostrophised some peasant girl: "Unhappy maid, how great your error! Ah! for your own sake and happiness shun the hateful thought of leaving your parents and the cottage where you were born! If you but knew the price they pay, those you envy, for silk and jewels with which they bedeck themselves!" "Ten francs a night!" Anais would interrupt. "I think that's what they get in Paris!"[9]

The last rejoinder in its fictional context is a small act of bravado, a shared pretence of sexual sophistication – but it also effectively demolishes the coyness of the textbook's rhetoric and asserts the reality of the girls' position. The only possible way to real wealth was through selling themselves, in or out of marriage, to a rich man.

The wit and irreverence of Colette's schoolgirls imply that female identity is not constructed solely by the discourse of the dominant ideology. It also suggests that a creative contradiction was at play here: on the one hand the extension of State education created effective channels for the transmission of a repressive ideology, but on the other hand it gave girls the legal right to an existence and an identity outside the home. Though girls had been attending primary schools in smaller numbers long before the advent of the Third Republic, the new laws made school attendance their right, defining them outside their role in the family, and thus providing some small measure of freedom and the possibility, however limited, of making a living in commercial or clerical work, or even as a school teacher, thus escaping peasant life. Claudine's classmates, between them, take up all these possibilities.

Nine years at the village school thus provided Colette with an explicit formulation of patriarchal attitudes and an experience of shared freedom that partially subverted them. This ambiguous experience was shared by the majority of her female contemporaries, but it was compounded in Colette's case by a further contradiction between the ideology of gender inscribed in the syllabus and that of her lived experience at home.

Outwardly, the Colette family conformed to the social norms of the day. There was some slight aura of scandal over the years 1860–65, for when the ex-soldier Captain Colette came to take up the post of tax collector in Saint-Sauveur, his wife-to-be was still married to her drunken, solitary first husband Jules Robineau-Duclos, by whom she had a daughter, Juliette. The newcomer and the lonely young woman soon formed a friendship, and the village gossiped about the paternity of Sido's second child Achille, born in 1863. But when Robineau-Duclos died in 1865, leaving his wife a comfortable fortune, Sido and Captain Colette married and set up home together, and by the time Sidonie Gabrielle was born in 1873 the household appeared unexceptional. Captain Colette was the wage-earner and managed the family finances: Sido looked after the house and the four children.

The conventional division of roles though, concealed a more complex reality. The view of gender, of sexual morality and even of maternity, signified by life in the

Colette household conflicted with the dominant ideology in several ways. Sido's own background was sufficiently unconventional to have allowed her a detached perspective on the social practices of the French bourgeoisie. Having lost her mother early Sido had a variety of homes and spent the latter part of her girlhood living with her two older brothers, both journalists, in Belgium "amongst painters, journalists and musicians" (*Sido*, 155). Having no dowry, she had been obliged to accept the first willing and viable suitor who came along, but marriage with the dissolute Robineau-Duclos brought her no closer to a conventionally bourgeois lifestyle. Sido's life began to fit a more typically domestic pattern after her second marriage, but her attitudes and behaviour remained eccentric in the context of late nineteenth-century France.

There is a problem in writing of the Sido whose love and view of the world formed the central influence in her daughter's early life, for almost all the evidence we have is precisely that of her daughter, whose creation she in turn became. The "Sido" of Colette's writing is the mother figure constructed by an adult Colette, and to take the written text as mere biographical evidence is to ignore the retrospective and creative aspect of autobiographical writing. The danger of confusing Sido as historical person with Colette's creation "Sido" needs to be acknowledged, but must also be confronted if we are to pursue the question of contradictory ideologies in Colette's early childhood.

Although the figure of "Sido" will be considered as part of Colette's literary creation, there is also sufficient external evidence to justify reference to the unconventional Sido as a historical character, for in the letters she wrote to her daughter the beliefs and attitudes attributed to her by Colette appear to be very much her own – and those attitudes were certainly not those of the virtuous wife and mother projected by the official discourse of the age.

The good woman of the Republic's rhetoric was centred

in the domestic world of the home, and her work there valued because it supported and maintained the working male population. Economically and emotionally women's role was an auxiliary one: the mother evoked in the textbooks loved, encouraged, patiently cared for the children and husband who were the actual or future protagonists in the social world. In a study of one of the most widely used French language textbooks of the early Third Republic, Dominique Maingeneau examines those grammar sentences governed by the subject "the mother" and (though Maingeneau's concerns have nothing to do with gender) finds that they are entirely consistent. Every clause cited signifies the mother's self-abnegation and primary concern for the child who is characterised as male by the gender of the word "enfant": the mother is devoted, kind, anxious about her child's health; she cares for her child, forgives, guides his first steps, waits patiently.[10]

The good woman thus implicitly acknowledged her secondary status. It followed that – as in Freud's scenario of emotional development – the successful maturing of the male subject depended on his leaving behind the maternal order, with its lack of autonomy and its social limitations, for the greater satisfactions of the paternal order. Spatially, this structure was frequently represented by locating the mother within a romanticised home, far from the site of adult, male activity, a home which the son had to leave behind in order to become a man and which he then remembered fondly as the source of his manly ideals.

Thus in the textbook cited above Louis Pasteur returns as a national hero to the humble home of his childhood and recalls how his mother inspired him with enthusiasm for science; in a collection of extracts from great French authors also studied by Maingeneau – published in 1905, after Colette's schooldays, but representative of a system of values that remained fairly constant throughout the period 1871–1914 – George Washington's story is told in terms of his mother's selfless devotion and her inspiration of her son's patriotism. Washington, about to become President of the United States, returns for one last visit to the cottage where his old mother still lives – and where she then dies, once her son has returned to the capital and achieved glory.[11] The subordination of the mother's selfhood to her inspirational, nurturing role translates neatly into spatial and narrative form.

It is significant, too, that the location of the mother's home tends to be rural. In a society that defined itself in terms of rationality, whose predominant philosophy was that of positivism with its belief in man's capacity to understand, quantify and hence control the material world, the town was the natural site of progress and the country linked to notions of regression and traditionalism. This was also a society on the road to industrialisation, which further defined the rural world as backward and outside the real thrust of history. The positioning of women within the natural world followed from this structure of thought: women, like the countryside, were necessary, pleasurable and in the background, outside the major developments of the social world. Thus the figure of the devoted mother is often also tucked away in some idyllic hamlet, the source, but not the location of her son's glory.

In a sense, the Sido of Colette's writing fits this figurative linking of women and nature: she is more interested in her garden than in politics, immensely knowledgeable about the natural world, prefers the provinces to Paris, and is skilled in the domestic arts of growing and preparing food. But though in a material and an emotional sense Sido was a nurturing mother and an able housewife, her relationship to husband, children and domestic labour reads as significantly different from that constructed by the school syllabus or the rhetoric of the period. Sido's identification with the natural world reverses the significance of the woman–nature equation. In the representations of maternity discussed above, women and nature are linked by their subordination to the rational, urban, public world of men. Their role is an auxiliary and a functional one: they ensure the reproduction of the workforce and of "great men" by giving birth, feeding and servicing the nation. In Colette's texts on childhood Sido's attitudes to motherhood and to domestic work implicitly deny the auxiliary status of these activities, and her nurturing relationship to her children has little to do with the selfless devotion and sense of social duty the textbooks prescribe. Nature, rather than nation, must be treated with respect and children receive the freedom of their parents' "deliberate and considered refusal to interfere" (*Sido*, 183). Sido's pride in her children is based less on their social accomplishments than on their physical beauty, health and independence. It is a sensual, admiring love that includes a sense of pleasure in her own creativity:

> She let go of my rein of hair and stood away from me so as to see me better. "Go and show them what I can produce!" (*Sido*, 161)

> She gazed at her two boys, the half-brothers, and found them beautiful. (*Sido*, 183)

The nature of Sido's endearments confirm the emphasis on her physical delight in her children: Gabrielle is her "jewel of pure gold", her "beauty", her "golden sun".

Sido's attitude to domestic work repeats this negation of women's work as service: some forms of work are necessary and pleasurable, like the preparation of food, or tending the garden, though here pleasure can take precedence over necessity so that the functional nature of the work is denied. Thus she makes a scarecrow to scare the birds away from the cherries, but stands watching in delight as one bold blackbird ignores it and eats the fruit.

Reminded by her child that the cherries were to be for the family, Sido returns to her maternal identity:

> "The cherries? Yes, of course, the cherries!" In those eyes there flickered a sort of wild gaiety, a contempt for the whole world, a light-hearted disdain which cheerfully spurned me along with everything else. (*Sido*, 156)

Other types of work are acknowledged as necessary but are not pleasurable, and here a wilder and less patient Sido emerges beneath the housekeeper.

> . . .though she was active and always on the go, she was not a sedulous housewife . . . With a flannel in her hands, and one eye on the servant dawdling over her window-cleaning and smiling at the man next door, she would utter nervous exclamations like impatient cries for freedom. (*Sido*, 143)

The difference does not lie in the activities undertaken, but in their definition as peripheral, as necessary but minor infringements of a freedom which is much more central to the mother's identity.

The negation of the image of selfless mother extends too to spatial definition. Whilst in the texts on childhood Sido is centrally located in the home or garden, her relation to surrounding space is not at all that of the textbooks' devoted mother. In the scenario created by the latter, the space beyond the domestic circle is defined as masculine. The mother may empower her son to enter that world by teaching him the skills and principles appropriate there, but knowledge and power beyond the home are a male affair and once he leaves the maternal space she must remain in the background of grateful memory.

Sido not only negates this structure by her movements, for she took regular trips to Paris and returned with stories, purchases, gifts but also, in her daughter's reconstruction of childhood, erases the boundary between inner, female space and outer, male-defined space: she is represented as the centre of a Mariner's Chart or rose, able to read the signs of the natural world so that she can predict rain or frost, encouraging her children, and especially the youngest female child, to explore and observe the world freely. The garden fences are never quite standing in Sido's garden, always falling down or "grappling in mid-air with the invincible arms of a hundred years old wisteria" (*MMH*, 23) so that they fail to separate the garden from the world outside. Images of stars, ripples and concentric circles signify that Sido's power is not limited to a small world which must be left behind in the pursuit of knowledge and maturity, but that it radiates outward, encompassing not only the natural but also the social world.

For unencumbered by a conventional sense of propriety or reverence, Sido interprets cultural and social signs with the same acute perceptiveness she applies to natural signs. The historical Sido was unawed, though voraciously curious, before the attractions of Paris, quite able to encompass the adult Colette's unorthodox lifestyle within her generous scheme of values:

> . . . Even though I've always thought sharing a bed with one's husband was not a very nice or proper thing to do, putting whole streets between yourself and him does seem a little much . . .[12]

she commented with mild irony, on Colette's departure from the marital home.

Sexual morality had always been one of Sido's more unorthodox areas: in a peculiarly modern way she failed to understand why it was better for a pregnant girl to marry a mean or unattractive husband than to have her child alone: "after all a lovely, unrepentant creature, big with child, is not such an outrageous sight" (*Sido*, 123), so that the family's maid, on more than one occasion, was a pregnant girl whom no-one else would employ. Nor did Sido ever consider it natural that her daughters should go off to share a house with some male stranger simply on the grounds that he had been legally transformed into a husband.

> "I've had enough of this perpetual anxiety over my daughters. Already the eldest has gone off with that man . . ."
> "How, gone off?"
> "Oh, well, married him if you prefer it. Married or not married, she has none the less gone away with a man whom she hardly knows."
> She gave my father a look full of loving suspicion.
> "And after all, you, what have you to do with me? You aren't even a relation!" (*MMH*, 42)

Her own loving, even passionate relationship with her second husband seems to have involved little recognition of the authority the law granted him, on either side.

Colette grew up in a society that was clearly and overtly patriarchal outside the home, but the seamless coherence of patriarchy was flawed, firstly by the double-edged experience of a female education, and secondly by the unorthodox attitudes of her mother. The dominant ideology, however, was not merely a set of ideas to be dismissed: it was grounded in the material reality of male economic and political power. When Gabri, as her mother called her, reached her late teens everything – economic constraints, social expectations, sexual desire – led her to accept marriage as the means of transition to adulthood. On 15 May 1893, in Chatillon, Sidonie Gabrielle Colette married Henry Gauthier-Villars, or Willy: friend of the Colette family, writer and journalist, and notorious Parisian *bon viveur*. The move to Paris meant the beginning of a more lonely and difficult life, but also the entry into a milieu where writing was an accepted means of making a living.

3 Claudine in Context

Photographs of Willy and his young bride bring to mind the union of Beauty and the Beast: she was slight, very young, physically appealing, while he was stout and balding and looked closer to fifty than thirty. His attitude to the marriage was only cautiously positive: as he explained in a letter to his brother, he was still mourning the death of his mistress, the mother of his son, and whilst he found the Colettes' daughter "charming" he was marrying her partly out of gratitude for their kindness to himself and the motherless child, who had been fostered out near Chatillon. The flat into which the couple moved in Paris was dark and sunless, decorated obsessively by a previous tenant with thousands of tiny pieces of coloured paper stuck on to every available surface. Gabrielle had left behind the warm, abundant space of the maternal world and found herself alone in an environment that was radically, painfully different. The forests and flowers of Burgundy were replaced by the streets of Paris, Sido's loving attention by Willy's frequent indifference and soon by his infidelities, and the sheer powerlessness of a young woman in a deeply patriarchal society became an acute reality without the counterbalance of Sido's alternative values.

The change was hard enough to make her physically ill: in 1894 Sido was called to Paris to nurse her daughter back to health. Yet in her written reconstruction of this period (*Mes Apprentissages* [*My Apprenticeships*] 1936) Colette's depiction of Willy is ironic rather than bitter.

> My life as a woman began with that jouster. It was a very serious encounter for a village girl. Before him

> everything – except my parents' ruin, and the furniture being publicly sold off – was roses. But what would I have done with a life of nothing but roses? (*MA*, 21)

Marriage, for all its miseries, represented for a young woman virtually the only means of entering a wider adult world. Though in the late nineteenth century girls were supposed to be innocently chaste, Colette also emphasises the factor of sexual desire and curiosity in the will to marry.

> Aided by my youth and ignorance, I started off in a state of intoxication – guilty intoxication, driven by the dreadful, impure urges of adolescence. (*MA*, 29)

And Willy was not only the Beast, he was cultured, witty and worldly-wise, and on the evidence of Colette herself and of the numbers of women who found him attractive, he possessed a charm that the photographs fail to convey. Above all he introduced Gabrielle into a world where writing was a common practice and an accepted means of earning a living. Through Willy, Gabrielle became Colette, not only in the sense that he chose to address her by her family name, thus introducing a variation on the re-naming of women by their husbands, but also in the sense that he discovered, and exploited, her ability as a writer.

The milieu Colette entered by marrying Willy occupied a borderland between the salon society of the ruling class and the more Bohemian, licentious *demi-monde*. By birth and family connections Willy had access to the most respectable society. By profession and inclination he was also part of the "half world" of high-class prostitutes, writers struggling to make a living, artists and entertainers. It was through men like Willy that the two circles came to intersect: as in Zola's *Nana* (1880), set some thirty years earlier, the double standard of sexual morality meant that men of the ruling class could move between the two worlds without transgressing rules of masculine behaviour, whilst women were less socially mobile.

But though he was thoroughly reactionary in political terms, Willy's observance of social convention seems to have been only partial and pragmatic, and thus, as his wife Colette did find herself both in the salons of the rich and powerful, and in the cafés and houses frequented by the kept women upon whose sexual services the maintenance of the double standard depended. The two worlds in fact mirrored and complemented each other, despite the superficial radicalism of the *demi-monde*, with its tolerance of deviant sexuality and its relaxation of class boundaries. Moving between them Colette could observe different modes of female dependence, for if the society hostesses depended on husbands for their name, their income and their status, the *cocottes* had to frankly advertise their qualities as objects of desire and symbols of wealth. It was they who took the uncomfortable fashions of the day to their extremes as they squeezed themselves into long, wasp-waisted corsets and narrow high-heeled shoes, forcing their breasts and hips into an exaggerated representation of the female body. But Colette was also able to observe strategies of resistance, from the verbal debunking of male power she attributes in *My Apprenticeships* to Caroline Otero:

> "Remember [she said] there is always a moment in the life of a man – even a miser – when he really opens his hand wide."
> "The moment of passion?"
> "No. The moment when you twist his wrist." (*MA*, 12)

to the rejection of heterosexuality in favour of lesbianism. Sapphism, as female homosexuality was also known, was an acknowledged practice in both circles and was tolerated to the extent that it was perceived as non-threatening. Whilst it could be seen as merely compensatory, or enjoyed as a spectacle for male voyeurism, lesbianism could be allowed to exist in the margins of a heterosexual culture. But the choice of another woman as partner and as object of desire was also potentially subversive, a point demonstrated in 1907 by the scandalised hostility that greeted Colette's own public liaison with the Marquise de Morny, "Missy".

Beyond the world of the salons women were developing other strategies to challenge the male monopoly of power: though their participation in the French trade-union movement and in strike action was limited, the early years of this century saw a gradual increase in the unionisation of women and a small but significant number of women-only strikes. 1878 to 1913 was the great era of feminist congresses in France, most of them organised by middle-class women and reformist in aim, but setting out an agenda of fundamental change towards economic and social equality. Though politics remained a world apart for Colette and for most of the women she frequented, the political feminists were equally engaged with the production of written texts in these years. Publishing was a major feminist activity in 1900: between 1871 and 1914 thirty-five different feminist papers appeared in France, and Marguerite Durand's successful *La Fronde* appeared as a daily between 1897 and 1903, running campaigns for birth control, for the suppression of the prostitution laws that criminalised only women, for the vote and for equal pay.

Both the milieux frequented by Willy and Colette were literary: in this period of economic prosperity with Paris one of the great cultural centres of the Western world, publishing was a lucrative and an expanding business. Willy made a living by writing music reviews and gossip columns for the mass of newspapers and magazines fashionable at the time and also by employing an army of ghost-writers to produce punning, titillating light novels which he published under his own name. Colette recalled with affection many of the young men who worked for her husband and who became her friends, and it was almost inevitable that an unoccupied and literate young wife, already financially dependent and hence a source of cheap labour, should herself have been drawn into the production process.

From the earliest years of the marriage she collaborated in the writing of reviews and articles, and the story of how she came to write fiction has become a central element of the Colette myth. Convalescent after her illness, she was asked by Willy to write down her memories of schoolgirl life. At first unimpressed, Willy later recognised the commercial potential of the product he had elicited, and after a little stylistic improvement and the addition of some mild eroticism, succeeded in getting *Claudine at School* published under the sole name Willy in 1900. It was a runaway success, and was followed by sequels in 1901 (*Claudine in Paris*), 1902 (*Claudine Married* [*Claudine en ménage*]), 1903 (*Claudine and Annie* [*Claudine s'en va*]), and finally by *The Retreat from Love* (*La Retraite sentimentale*) in 1907, after the couple's separation and under the name Colette Willy. Accompanied by stage versions of the book, by the sale of *Claudine* products such as collars, perfumes, even toothpicks and by Willy's self-publicising outings with Colette herself and Polaire, the stage Claudine, both dressed in the style of the new cult heroine, the Claudine books were a commercial success in the manner of some present day children's fiction. Two novels about another young heroine, Minne, also appeared under Willy's name in 1904 and 1895.

Colette's first works of literature were thus not in any direct sense confessional, or autobiographical. Though the close similarities between the biography of author and character are undeniable, these novels were produced not out of a desire for self-expression, but in response to the demands of a man on whom Colette depended: they were aimed at the market rather than at an intimate audience. Writing from the outset signified self-production rather than communication of feeling, and the quite sophisticated narrative strategies of the often maligned early novels confirm this. It is by setting them against the work of other contemporary women novelists that we can best see the *Claudine* and *Minne* novels as both products of their age and as innovatory in ways that foreshadow Colette's work as an independent writer.

Claudine begins her textual life aged fifteen and ends it five novels later, around the age of thirty. Apart from in *Claudine and Annie*, the fourth book, she is narrator as well as central protagonist, and the world is focalised largely through her perceptions. *Claudine at School* centres on the school in her native village of Montigny, and on Claudine's education, both academic and in the broader sense of the word. *Claudine in Paris* brings the country girl to the city in time-honoured literary tradition, and narrates her meeting with the seductive older man Renaud whose proposal of marriage closes the novel.

Claudine Married begins a year and a half after the wedding but narrates analeptically (or in flashback) the start of their marriage, before proceeding to the central episode, that of Claudine's affair with a woman friend Rezi, and of Renaud's curiously perverse complicity. It ends with Claudine alone, though awaiting the return of Renaud, in the garden of Montigny. *Claudine and Annie* (more significantly entitled *Claudine Goes Away* in the original French) changes narrative voice and focus taking the form of a diary written by Annie who begins the novel as a submissive wife anxious to observe the wishes of her absent husband, and ends it about to depart alone on an independent, vagabond journey. Her friendship with Claudine, here seen in the third person apart from one letter she writes to Annie, is an important factor in the latter's transformation. Finally *The Retreat from Love*, which does not wholly belong in this consideration of Colette's "Willy" period, brings Claudine and Annie together again in Claudine's own narration and ends after the death of Renaud with Claudine again alone, in voluntary exile, in a garden that represents the natural world and retreat into the self.

If Willy saw commercial possibilities in the *Claudine* novels it was because he was aware of the contemporary climate in publishing, and of what was selling. The works of fiction published under his own name in the 1890s demonstrate his belief that sex sold books: they mainly centre on a series of erotic encounters between a male protagonist and a voracious woman whose sexual appetite threatens his identity and his potential as an artist. The perspective of the *Claudine* series is of course very different, but the accentuation of the erotic theme produces a degree of continuity between these novels and those previously signed by Willy.

The *Claudine* novels' central structure, however, that of a rural, *ingénue* heroine making the transition from childhood to womanhood in a society she only partially understands, also had a recent literary precedent. In 1894 Gyp – penname of the aristocratic Sybille de Riquetti de Mirabeau – had had considerable success with the novel *Le Mariage de Chiffon*. *Chiffon* is a light romantic novel in which the teenage heroine succeeds in avoiding the undesirable suitors proposed by a cynically materialist mother, and finds a happy ending in the arms of her handsome step-uncle. The narrative is enlivened by the heroine's guileless candour: with childlike sincerity she ignores the unspoken codes and the polite deceptions of her society, and articulates what they conceal. Refusing one rich and prestigious suitor on the grounds that she really does not feel able to reach the level of hypocrisy demanded of a bourgeois wife, she comments: "I'm really no good at being nice to people I can't stand; I don't know how to make fools believe I think they're witty – and if I married you I'm sure I'd be unfaithful" (*MC*, 117).

The heroine's sharp-tongued innocence, her combination of a slightly transgressive boyishness with very feminine beauty, the Oedipal overtones of marriage with a much older man, all have a piquancy that appealed to contemporary readers and all link this text to the *Claudine* series. There is a further similarity in the association of the heroine with a natural, rural world: Chiffon's innocence and energy are implicitly opposed to the corruption of the city: "I'm not a woman, I'm a savage . . . made to live with flowers and animals" (*MC*, 117). This structure also recurs in other contemporary novels and notably in Marcelle Tinayre's *Hellé*, published in 1898.

Gyp was almost thirty years older than Colette and already a prolific and well-known writer by the time Colette met her in Paris. Marcelle Tinayre was much closer in age – born in 1871 – and was beginning a long and illustrious career as a journalist and novelist. She and Colette were to become friends and their names were often linked in later years when reviewers referred to the leading women writers of the day. In Tinayre's *Hellé* the orphaned heroine, classically educated in a rural retreat by a male guardian scornful of contemporary values, is brought to Paris to confront the modern world and, inevitably, to discover romantic love. The narrative leads down a number of false trails as handsome and charming suitors turn out to have no moral fibre, until at last Hellé discovers a worthy partner who shares her concern for social reform and moral authenticity. Like Chiffon, Hellé ends the novel in the arms of an exceptionally lovable hero.

Despite their dependence on the familiar narrative pattern of romantic fiction, both of these novels by women contain some mild questioning of gender roles. Though the central question posed and answered by the plot is the question of romance: whom will she marry?, narrative and theme are enriched by a further question. How can the heroine's demand for emotional and sexual fulfilment be met when marriage is her only realistic destiny, yet represents the exchange of her freedom for security and dependence? In Chiffon's case, the problematic nature of marriage becomes apparent through the characterisation of the heroine as a tomboyish, outspoken child to whom feminine codes of dress and behaviour clearly represent restrictions, and through the failure of most of her suitors to match her in mental or physical energy. In *Hellé*, a more serious and expository novel, the question is raised quite explicitly. Like Chiffon, Hellé views her society from the perspective of an outsider, armed with the authentic values which the novel associates with the natural world of her childhood. She thus finds the definition of the wifely role as one of "gentleness, sacrifice, submission" (*H*, 230) quite unacceptable, and formulates her objections:

> Why should the woman sacrifice herself rather than the man? Why should I obliterate my personality because I love someone? A man unjust enough to demand my intellectual suicide would be a tyrant or a fool, and I certainly couldn't love him. (*H*, 230)

A significant sub-plot also sees Hellé finding ways to help an unmarried mother whose plight formed the subject of several other contemporary texts by women (*Marie Fille-Mère* by Lucie Delarue – Mardrus, for example, published in 1908).

Such expressions of dissent, however, are rapidly recuperated within the narratives themselves. The problematic question of a conflict between female aspiration and social reality is resolved by means of the exceptional hero: if marriage figures as a threat to female autonomy, it is redeemed by the appearance of a husband whose authority is benevolent and who shares the heroine's high moral standards. The heroes of both novels are considerably older than the heroines, which accentuates their authority, and are distinguished from their rival suitors by the fact that they are, in some loosely defined way, engaged in social reform. This both situates them with the heroine above contemporary society, and suggests that the latter may be reformed from within, averting any implied need for radical solutions.

At the same time each novel operates a change of perspective on the heroine which transforms signifiers of independence into signifiers of passive sexuality. *Chiffon*, with its extra-diegetic narrator emphasises the heroine's suppleness, agility, good health and "rosy cheeks, dishevelled hair" through most of the text, but suddenly adopts the perspective of the hero in the novel's closing scene to describe Chiffon "immobile in the centre of the room, all pink in her filmy dress that flowed down over her hips, moulding the delicate lines of her young, vigorous little body" (*MC*, 285). *Hellé*, a first person narrative, closes with a similar device as Hellé implicitly assumes Antoine's perspective to describe their final embrace in terms of the most conventional imagery: "And I was in Antoine's arms. He was holding ... his virginal prey, at last vanquished and won" (*H*, 284).

A far more radical interrogation of gender appeared in the fiction of Rachilde, hostess of one of the literary salons attended by Willy and Colette, literary critic of the prestigious *Mercure de France* owned by her husband Alfred Vallette, and the first reviewer to imply that the author of the *Claudine* novels might have been Madame rather than Monsieur Willy. Rachilde's curiously ghoulish fiction, set in exotically furnished apartments far from the light of day, belongs to a *fin-de-siècle* literary current of Decadence, which also encompassed much of the work of Willy's ghost-writers Marcel Schwob and Jean de Tinayre.

The Decadents were characterised by a rejection of the natural world and a revulsion from the pragmatic materialism of the Third Republic. Aloof from society and from nature, they took refuge in an art which was to replace rather than represent the material and social world, and "(accorded) aesthetic primacy . . . to the strange and the artificial".[1] They were almost all men and followed Baudelaire in identifying despised nature with woman, characterising her as the embodiment of both triviality and base materiality. Sexuality could only be redeemed by separation from the "natural", by being channelled into the more cerebral pleasure of the erotic. In their rejection of the natural world, and in their elitist intellectual stance, the Decadents could not have been more different from Colette. In terms of the importance attributed to the natural world she is much closer to the lyrical women poets of the *belle époque*, Anna de Noailles whose first collection of poetry *Le coeur innombrable* was published in 1900, Lucie Delarue-Mardrus and Renée Vivien.

Yet in writing from a female perspective Rachilde gave the eccentric and finally sterile conventions of Decadence an unexpected dimension. Rachilde's dramas revolve around powerful and frustrated women who impose strange wills on the male protagonists, reversing the norms of gender relationships and thereby opening them to question. The narratives may limp a little, for between the first meeting of the two main characters, and the final destruction of one or the other, there are only a series of repeatedly unsatisfied sexual encounters, often narrated in such equivocal terms that it is quite hard to decide what exactly, in physical terms, is supposed to be happening! But in the radical reversal of roles there is an oblique commentary on the norms of patriarchy. Raoule de Vénérande in the notorious *Monsieur Venus* (1888) reduces her male "mistress" to a passive and mistreated instrument of pleasure and having finally brought about his death replaces him, with ghastly symbolism, by a mechanical dummy bearing the dead lover's own hair, teeth and nails.

La Jongleuse (*The Juggler*, 1900) refuses the arrogant Leon as lover, preferring as objects of sexual desire the exotic vase that stands in her room and the knives with which she juggles and at last kills herself: here the man is both reduced to and rejected as object of desire, in ironic mimicry of the Decadent stance.

The perspective of female desire also produces some unusually sensual description of the male body. Raoule, voyeur-like, spies on Jacques as he bathes, observing:

> the small of his back, where the spine vanished into a voluptuous plane and rose again into two firm, plump, adorable curves . . . (*MV*, 59)

There is a displacement of gender signs on several levels; in Jacques' activity of silk flower making in the opening chapter and in the silky robes he wears later in the novel; in Raoule's designation by masculine nouns and adjectives even as she is desired by the other male protagonist, Raittolbe; in Leon's dream in *La Jongleuse*, where Eliante becomes a phallic column of smoke whirling to the heavens and he regrets, still dreaming, the fact that he has "no revolver or toy gun to hand" with which to shoot the column down and "reduce female importance" (*LaJ*,128).

Different as the two writers are, in the shifting of conventional gender signs and the thematic importance implicitly accorded to definitions of the masculine and the feminine, Rachilde prefigures Colette. Their mutual admiration for each other's writing confirms this: not only did Rachilde praise *Claudine at School* as "the most extraordinary work to blossom from the pen of a new writer" in which "woman, at the height of puberty, cries out her instincts, her desires, her wishes and . . . her crimes",[2] but in 1904 Colette also published a very positive review of Rachilde's novel *Tour d'amour*.

The *Claudine* novels then, brought together several features of the period's popular fiction and their success can partly be explained by the fact that they corresponded to a contemporary climate of feeling. However, the degree of their success, and their lasting interest, also require explanation in terms of originality and difference. Despite their author's criticism of the "lack of skill" they reveal and of her own excessive "ease in accomplishing what was asked of me" (*MA*, 72–3), the novels do possess distinct qualities that distinguish them clearly from the fiction described above.

They are for one thing, peculiarly open-ended. Novels by Colette's female contemporaries in the early 1900s may have been varied in theme and in tone, but they tended to share a narrative structure that centred on the possibility of an authentic relationship, and closed with its achievement (Tinayre, Gyp) or with the death of one of the protagonists (Rachilde, Delarue-Mardrus in *Marie Fille-Mère*). The implication of this repeated structure is that the alternatives for women lie in romantic love, or in death: the closure of the narrative signifies the closing off of other possibilities.

Like so many features of these early novels, the absence of closure in the *Claudine* volumes is in part determined by Willy's eye for the market – the possibility of sequels must be maintained. But it also means that the novels imply a less linear pattern to women's lives. *Claudine at School* ends with the ending of Claudine's schooldays, but the comic climax to the sub-plot of adult sexual intrigues offsets Claudine's sense of loss and concludes the novel on a forward-looking, humorous note. *Claudine in Paris*, it is true, observes a more traditional pattern by ending with Renaud's proposal of marriage, but since *Claudine Married* then begins with the words "There is surely something wrong with our marriage", the sense of marriage as closure is limited to the single volume. *Claudine Married* concludes with a reaffirmation of the relationship with Renaud, but this is undermined by the character's absence from the concluding pages and the fact that Claudine declares her return to Montigny to be definitive: the commitment to Renaud is contradicted by a renewed commitment to her single, and by implication more authentic, identity.

Claudine and Annie operates a radical reversal of the structure of *Claudine in Paris*, and of the structure of the romantic novel: instead of charting the meeting of hero and heroine and their progression to the conclusion of marriage, this novel starts with a married couple and traces the wife's gradual rediscovery of a single identity, concluding with her departure. *The Retreat from Love* is the least structured of the five, in a narrative sense, for it is a novel of waiting and of conversation, ending with the death of a Renaud who has, in any case, been absent for most of the novel. Though this is the last episode in Claudine's story, the final vision of her in the garden at Montigny does not close her story in any definitive way – for throughout the sequence Montigny has been a place of retreat and renewal, enabling the heroine to engage in further action.

The characteristic tone of the *Claudine* books is one of agreeable irreverence, and this too distinguishes them from the earnestly rhetorical stance of a Tinayre or a Delarue-Mardrus, the arch complicity of Gyp or the satanic tones of Rachilde. The difference has much to do with narrative perspective: Claudine's diary-like first person, with frequent use of the present tense, positions the reader with the narrator, rather than as observer and invites the reader to share Claudine's acute and often comical perceptions of her society and its cast of characters. Gyp and Tinayre may invite the reader to sympathise with their heroines' questioning of social norms, but they limit the impact of her critique by defining the heroine as naive, in Gyp's case by the use of a third person narrative which joins reader and implied author in a perspective of maturity that excludes the heroine. Tinayre's *Hellé* is told in the first person, but retrospectively in the French past historic tense which has a distancing effect. There is irony in the narrator's recollection of her younger self:

> At that celestial hour, in what street of the city . . . was he awakening, the lover of my dreams . . . When would I meet him? By what mysterious sign would I know him? (*H*, 36)

In the case of Rachilde the reader is distanced by the radical strangeness of the heroine and by a narrative perspective that observes her, for the most part externally. Claudine, however, is not defined as naive: her broad reading and familiarity with nature have given her a perfectly adequate sex education, and we rarely observe her from any perspective other than her own. The reader shares in her precise and gleeful deflation of men and institutions.

Humour, of a sharp-witted but rarely cruel variety, is an important component of the *Claudine* series. Serious about the natural world, with which she identifies her deepest pleasures, serious too as the sequence progresses, about her love for Renaud, Claudine is for the rest a narrator who delights in the absurd and the comic. The novels contain a rich cast of original comic characters: from her father, so preoccupied with his treaty on the molluscs of the region that he rarely remembers the world outside his study, emerging occasionally in the first two volumes only to hum a bawdy song or fail to recognise his relatives; to Anais of the impassive face and the dervish dances, with her penchant for eating the school's stationery supplies, and to the garishly dressed Marthe of *Claudine and Annie*, who imprisons her writer-husband every day until he produces the required amount of words (nicely reversing Colette's own plight).

The humour sharpens when it is directed at the powerful, as in *Claudine at School* where the pompous rhetoric of the Third Republic is the object of Claudine's caustic wit. Asked to write an essay on "Franklins's observation that idleness is like rust, it is more wearing than hard work" (*CS*, 106) Claudine wearily enumerates the platitudes needed to gain a good mark:

> Here we go! And we'll have the comparison between the shiny key, rounded with regular use, and the key that's rusted away because no-one used it. The good labourer working away happily, risen at dawn, whose brawny muscles, etcetera . . . we'll have him compared to the idle man lounging on oriental divans etc; etc . . .[3]

Elsewhere she punctures the self-importance of the Examiners at her final exam by considering them for the reader, in physical terms: "mopping their brows, they're ugly and their skin's shiny with heat. Heavens! I wouldn't care to be married in weather like this!" (*CS*, 156–7). The visit of the Minister of Agriculture to Montigny to open the new school buildings is a wickedly observed exercise in deflation, from the arrival of the honoured guest ("a cross-looking little man with a stomach like a bullfinch" [*CS*, 200]) to Claudine's ironic commentaries on the words of the song the girls sing in his honour:

> Come arise! the day is dawning
> Honest toil demands our sweat!
> (If it's not content with the sweat of the official party, honest toil must demand a good deal!) (*CS*, 208)

Also present at the ceremonies is Dutertre, parliamentary candidate, self-appointed school visitor, and the first of the arrogant seducers to be ridiculed in the *Claudine* series. Dutertre is also a seductive character with his "wolf's teeth and dark eyes" (*CS*, 22), the only desirable male to enter the school premises and the object of the girls' fantasies. His abuse of power to gain sexual advantage is, however, punished in the final, farcical scene of *Claudine at School* as the schoolmistress's old mother finds him in bed with her daughter and, brandishing a broom, chases him from the house half-dressed to the delight of the dancers at the school ball. Claudine will respond in a similarly violent fashion when a well-dressed passer-by pinches her bottom on a Paris street:

> A leap in the air from Claudine, who raised her umbrella and brought it down on the gentleman's head, with typical Fresnois vigour. The gentleman's hat rolled in the gutter, to the immense delight of passers-by . . . (*CP*, 248)

In *The Retreat from Love* Annie recounts to Claudine several episodes in her search for sexual satisfaction but the funniest again creates, and ridicules, a sexually arrogant man, in this case the little tenor Rusinol who makes love at such speed that Annie is left quite unsatisfied and then rushes off to the piano to check that ejaculation has not damaged his high notes:

> That's how he spent his time! Jump on a woman, have her in five minutes and then quick, back to the piano to check it hadn't made his "C" go hoarse! (*RL*, 909)

says Annie, of the "imperious little cockerel who only cared for his own pleasure".

As narrator, and as character, Claudine is fully aware of sexual desire but apparently quite unaware of sexual morality in the conventional sense. This is very different from Tinayre's cautious questioning of a sexual morality that disadvantages women, or from Rachilde's explicitly transgressive role reversals. For Claudine sexual desire is a normal part of a girl's life, and the chaste and ignorant virgin of contemporary mythology is an alien creature. "It's odd" reflects Claudine in Paris "how since my illness my imagination and senses are quite chaste" (*CP*, 236), and Claudine's old nurse Melie, a sort of Chorus here, representing the authentic values of Montigny, is almost ready to find a lover for the good of Claudine's health, just as she locates a suitable Parisian tom for the cat Fanchette:

> . . . these last few days the poor love wanted it something cruel. She suffered for three whole days, so I asked round the neighbourhood, and the maid downstairs lent me a lovely husband for her, a striped grey tom. (*CP*, 256)

Claudine's passion for Renaud has elements of the romantic but is also intensely sexual:

> No man has ever kissed me on the mouth. His mouth is narrow but intense and the lower lip is full and round . . . I imagined his mouth, and the wildness in his darkened eyes, and a delightful anguish made me clasp my hands together. (*CP*, 363)

In *The Retreat from Love*, two modes of sexual behaviour are debated and compared at length, Claudine's passionate monogamy and Annie's promiscuous quest for "*la chair fraiche*" (young flesh). The terms of the debate are established rather than resolved, but the premise – that women's sexual desire is a vital force and its satisfaction to be taken seriously – is taken as read.

This positioning of female desire as central and as separable from romantic love, is in itself radical in the early

1900s. The erotic elements in the *Claudine* texts are often attributed to Willy's intervention for the manuscripts of the first two novels have disappeared making it impossible to establish precisely where he modified the text, and Colette tells us in *My Apprenticeships* that Willy insisted on some "spicing up" of her original text by the addition of lesbian affairs and girlish indiscretions. Willy was no doubt responsible for some of the more gratuitously titillating scenes, such as Claudine's recollection of the schoolgirls baring their breasts to see whose were the biggest in *Claudine in Paris*, a scene quite irrelevant to the narrative and clearly destined for the voyeur. However, the erotic aspect of the narratives is not simply grafted on by Willy, for in some ways it prefigures Colette's later work. And whilst the explicit narration of lesbian scenes may have been imposed, the extension of desire and of eroticised description across gender boundaries is an inherent part of the writing.

Throughout the novel cycle Claudine – and most of the other female characters – are presented as bi-sexual. To label them thus seems in a sense inappropriate since in the text they do not consciously belong to any sexual category but quite naturally perceive both male and female bodies as potential objects of desire. Claudine's lesbian affairs may bring emotional or practical problems, but they are never viewed as deviant. This absence of any rigorous division between homo- and hetero-sexuality, at least in the case of the female characters, means that the body is designated in the same precise and sensual language regardless of gender, and the conventional signifiers of gender are sometimes exchanged and displaced. Claudine writes of her young teacher's "supple body" (CS, 13) and of her "cat's eyes gleaming golden" (CS, 27), of the pleasure of "rest(ing) my head on her breast while she strokes my hair or my neck, and beneath my ear her heart beats fast" (*CS*, 27).

In the next volume it is on Renaud's shoulder that Claudine leans her head and his arms that enfold her, whilst Renaud's son Marcel, is described in the most feminine terms: "blond hair, a little long . . . a complexion like Luce's . . . He looks good enough to eat!" (*CP*, 244). The central event of *Claudine Married* is the affair with Rezi, characterised by curves and spirals, white skin and pale gold hair, but immediately preceding the development of the affair between the women comes a passage where Claudine contemplates the beauty of a male body in a painting in the Louvre:

> I should love to touch . . . the curving, brutal lips, and kiss those cynical page's eyes . . . that skin . . . the colour of old ivory at the groin and behind the knee . . . (*CM*, 439–40)

Claudine's own body, in that age of ample bosoms and wide hips, is "long, supple and muscular" with "firm hips, and almost no breasts" (*CM*, 414).

In emphasising the originality and the virtues of the *Claudine* novels, there is perhaps a danger of ignoring their very real flaws and of exaggeraing their radicalism. The novels also show signs of the author's youth and inexperience, and of the difficult personal and professional circumstances under which they were written. The character of Claudine herself becomes progressively more problematic as the protagonist created to enact schoolgirl adventures has to mature into a wife, a lover and then a widow. There is some contradiction between the attempt to maintain Claudine's distinctive, girlish charm (for the Claudine products were still on the market) and the development of her character into that of a reflective adult woman. This becomes particularly apparent in *Claudine and Annie*, when Claudine ceases to narrate and is seen instead in the third person. Unredeemed by her own self-mocking perspective, Claudine becomes an arch and rather ludicrous figure: Annie observes her wilfully refusing tea in the *salon de thé* where her friends are gathered, and persuading the ever indulgent Renaud to take her instead to drink cheap red wine in a down-market café:

> "Oh yes! Oh what fun!" cries the incorrigible Claudine. She looks at her husband with such childish enthusiasm, such loving admiration . . . (*C&A*, 561)

that Annie, the unloved, wants to cry but the reader is left slightly embarrassed by this display of kittenish charm in a woman well into her twenties.

The device of giving Annie the narrative voice in this fourth *Claudine* novel is no doubt itself a sign of Colette's difficulty in keeping Claudine alive. A degree of ambivalence had been there since *Claudine in Paris*, signified and more or less successfully resolved by various narrative devices. In *Claudine in Paris* the central structure of the narrative corresponds as we have seen, to that of romance, for Renaud gradually emerges as a figure of desirable and benevolent authority – in fact, as the hero – and Claudine ends the novel in his arms. There are, however, ironic parallels in the text which comment obliquely on this apparently happy resolution.

Renaud, as a sophisticated older man, echoes the wily Dutertre of *Claudine at School* though in a much improved version, and above all as Claudine's uncle by marriage he is linked to another, far less desirable uncle/lover in the story. Luce, Claudine's admirer and victim at the school in Montigny, has also found her way to Paris, but being penniless and homeless has become the mistress of the lecherous old uncle to whom she went for help. Whilst the emotional quality of the two relationships is very different, the exact paralleling of the two situations undermines the idealisation of Renaud as hero.

The decision to make Claudine a passionately faithful wife, with the exception of the affair with Rezi, introduces an idealised view of love that conflicts with the unregimented sensuality that is also part of Claudine's character. This also produces certain tensions in the text, as Claudine's fidelity is contradicted and questioned by Annie's discovery of pleasurable promiscuity. Claudine's commitment to Renaud becomes progressively more abstract and is expressed only through passages of dialogue and argument, as Renaud disappears from the narrative. Central only to *Claudine in Paris*, he appears intermittently in *Claudine Married* in the rather odd role of procurer, facilitating the affair with Rezi, and is absent from his own reunion with Claudine at the end, since this is signified only by a letter she writes to him.

The character of Renaud is merely peripheral in *Claudine and Annie*, and in *The Retreat from Love* he has suddenly become an old man whose failing health keeps him away in a sanatorium and out of the text until he returns briefly, to die. There is an attempt here to create the ideal male partner within the traditions of romance: strong, serene, protective and desirable. The contradictions that soon appear within the character, and his gradual effacement from the text, demonstrate the difficulties of constructing a romantic hero within the less conventional view of gender implied by the text as a whole.

The same tension between the polygamous imperatives of desire and a rather abstract respect for monogamy is present in the two *Minne* stories, first published in 1904 and 1905, but reworked and brought together in a single volume to be published under Colette's own name, and with the title *The Innocent Libertine (L'Ingénue libertine)*, in 1909. Minne is another *ingénue* heroine, but having been brought up, in contrast to Claudine, by an over-protective, deeply conventional mother, her adventurous spirit finds its outlet only in fantasy. On the basis of newspaper reports about the gang-leader Le Frise, she invents for herself a lean, lithe, criminal lover who will make her queen of the underworld. The perspective here is closer to the complicity between author and reader used in *Le Mariage de Chiffon*, for the stories are written in the third person and focalised partly through Minne, partly from the perspective of her adoring and gauche adolescent cousin Antoine, and partly by an extradiegetic narrator.

The reader is positioned with Minne in her desire for a "supple body, that smelt of lazy flesh and warm sand" (*IL*, 56) and in her irritation at the constrictions of her correct young life, but with Antoine in his awkward desire for Minne. A third, external perspective reveals the irony of their divergent desires and the unreality of Minne's fantasies. In the final episode of the first novel, Minne's daydreams become totally confused with the real world and she wanders the streets of Paris at night in search of Le Frise, her dream of a romantic encounter becoming in fact her pursuit by a lecherous old man, from whom she escapes to arrive home covered in mud, with her illusions shattered. The acute gap here between romantic fantasy and reality is resolved in a way that is satisfactory neither to the reader nor to Minne by marriage with Antoine, and the second half of *The Innocent Libertine* follows Minne through a frenetic series of sexual encounters in her attempt to find the sexual satisfaction she has failed to achieve with her husband:

> I bet it's his fault that I feel about as much pleasure as . . . as this seat. He must have wrenched something delicate inside me . . . (*IL*, 93)

Minne at last closes the novel having found satisfaction – in the arms of Antoine. The final scene of the novel has Minne in a hotel bedroom the morning after, contented and "nourished by the vanity of being a woman like other women" (*IL*, 187). Again, though, the narration has a certain ambivalence of tone, oscillating between Minne's own complacent perspective and an external perspective expressed in terms that signify loss rather than gain. Minne is scornful now of her yesterday's self, "that frigid child in quest of the impossible", for there is "no longer anything to search for" (*IL*, 187). Her gesture as she rubs her head against Antoine's sleeve is described as that of a "loving tame animal" and from her eyes "all the mystery has fled" (*IL*, 189).

The narrator hesitates between confirmation of the plot's central conclusion – that sexual satisfaction coincides with emotional fidelity – and a more subversive and open-ended meaning that includes regret for the doubting, seeking Minne destroyed by the ending. Colette reflected ruefully on the genesis of these fictions, on the short story all in "red, pink, black, some pale gold on the little heroine" with its mixture of "fantasy and *faits divers*" which she had written with pleasure, hoping to publish it under her own name and which Willy's bullying had extended to two novels that she never really liked again. "It is fortunate for the honour of the French novel that the end of my cowardice shortened the destiny of Minne and nipped in the bud God knows how many 'Minne in Hell', 'Daughter of Minne', 'Minne's Divorce' . . ." (*MA*, 126).

Radical, innovative, absorbing features of popular women's writing of the period whilst subverting many of their conventions, but also shot through with contradictions and uneven in quality, the early texts are very much worth reading and contain indications of what was to come when Colette slipped the leash, left the marital home and with it Willy's control and appropriation of her writing.

4 In the Crowd: Writing and the Social Order

Colette left Willy in 1906, at his suggestion. Her reluctance to make the break is understandable for divorce was still shocking and unusual in the early 1900s, and she had neither income nor reputation since Willy had appropriated the profits and the glory of the successful *Claudine* series. She survived with the support of Missy, the Marquise de Morny, her friend and lover until 1911, and through her own hard work and adaptability. She had already begun lessons in mime and appeared on the stage and at social functions: she now developed this interest into a career and made a living in the music-hall, partnered by her teacher Georges Waguc.

She also continued to write, using the signature "Colette Willy" under which two volumes of animal dialogues had already appeared, and quite rapidly achieved recognition: *The Vagabond* received three votes for the prestigious *Prix Goncourt* in 1910. Writing as a source of income meant not only books but also journalism, and it was through her articles for the newspaper *Le Matin* that Colette met the editor and future politician Henry de Jouvenel who became her lover, then her second husband and the father of her daughter Colette de Jouvenel, born in 1913 and nicknamed Bel Gazou.

Colette's career as journalist, essayist and novelist, as

well as her stage appearances in adaptations of her novels, continued throughout the years of her marriage to Jouvenel, and when they separated in 1923 she was an established literary figure, publishing under the sole name "Colette" and since 1920, a chevalier of the Legion of Honour. There was to be one more marriage, to her "best friend" (as she frequently refers to him) Maurice Goudeket, whom she met in 1925 and married ten years later, and a considerable amount of celebrity before her death in 1954. Despite protests from prominent Catholics like Graham Greene, the Church refused Colette a religious funeral, providing a final reminder that the Colette now adopted as a national figure had persistently flouted orthodox morality.

In a writing career extending over fifty years Colette produced a great quantity and variety of texts. The Fleuron *Complete Works* of 1950 did not include the whole of Colette's production, but ran nonetheless to fifteen large volumes of fiction, autobiographical essays, animal texts, newspaper articles, travel writing, film and theatre reviews, and lyrical prose that defies definition by genre. The popular image of Colette is a highly selective one which focuses on the most autobiographical elements of her fiction and on her writing about animals and nature, and thus perceives her as an intimately personal writer whose work is apolitical and whose only relevance to social history lies in her quaint evocations of the *belle époque*.

Yet whilst it is true that Colette's texts rarely represent the public world of politics, and adopt no overt political perspective, her writing is very much of and about its time, both in the sense that it includes a great deal of topical journalism (as the title of one volume of articles *In the Crowd* (*Dans la foule*, 1918) suggests), and in the sense that the narratives are firmly situated in a social and economic context. Colette's work does not divide neatly into discrete formal categories, for the "I" who addresses the reader from the pages of a newspaper on subjects of topical interest, shares the biography and the perspective of the "I" constructed within many of the stories and autobiographical texts. There is, nonetheless, a useful distinction to be made between the journalism, with its explicitly contemporary focus, and the literary texts with their more oblique relationship to historical circumstance. Both kinds of writing may be seen in terms of social relevance.

The music-hall is the setting for two of Colette's novels, *The Vagabond* and *Mitsou* (*Mitsou ou Comment l'esprit vient aux filles*, 1918), and for stories like "Bastienne's Child" and "Gribiche". It is also the subject of the short texts published for the most part, in *Le Matin* between 1909 and 1912 before being collected in the volumes *Tour Notes (Notes de tournées*, written c. 1909, published 1935) and *Music-hall Sidelights* (*L'Envers du music-hall*, 1913).

In these concise evocations of life on tour or in the popular theatres of Paris, Colette focuses on representative moments and characters, describing the arrival of the narrator and her companions at a brand new unfinished provincial theatre, or struggling through a cold early morning rehearsal. She then adopts an extradiegetic narrative voice to reveal five little dancers packed into a sordid dressing room and sewing as they await their turn to perform. The narrator, present or not on the "stage" of her text, adopts a tone of discreet and affectionate solidarity, apparent in the predominance of the "we" over the "I", in the willingness to take up the role of listener and to invite other artists to narrate their own stories, and in the warmth of descriptions like that of the girls in "The Workroom" who "in spite of their gaping wraps, of their high-pitched knees, of the insolent rouge still blossoming on their cheeks" have "the chaste attitude and bent backs of sedate seamstresses" (*CSC*, 119).

The music-hall is seen here as a good place to work because there is pleasure in performance and because the artists share a discreet but warm sense of comradeship. Colette's writing nevertheless emphasises the physical hardship beneath the glamour. Her dancers and acrobats are underpaid, underfed workers, their proletarian status emphasised by scenes where they mingle with their fellows:

> They jump on a bus, a tram, the underground, pell-mell with all the other employees – milliners, seamstresses, cashiers, typists – for whom the day's work is over. (*CSC*, 146)

and by direct analogy: one fellow dancer treats "Colette" "more as a colleague than a friendly companion, much as if we were workers in the same factory" (*CSC*, 128). In order to make ends meet the performers sew or "knit, everywhere and every minute, for a knitted garment shop" (*CSC*, 145), or they take middle-aged lovers who will set them up in a flat and pay the bills. Many of them are only a croissant away from starvation, like "The Starveling" (*CSC*, 122) or the young Bastienne who would faint in the dancing class for lack of food and pretend, for dignity's sake, that she was merely exhausted from a night with her lover (*CSC*, 112). The lack of food and rest does not make for good health, but since the body beautiful is their basic piece of professional equipment illness must be concealed.

The woman in "Journey's End", suffering from severe bronchitis and with the doctor's bills to pay "went on rehearsing with forty cups on my back" – "cups" being a contemporary form of heat treatment – "and so hid the fact I was suffering. When I was seized by a fit of coughing, I rushed off to the lav, otherwise they'd have replaced me within the hour, you bet!" (*CSC*, 141).

The ironic contrast between stage glamour and the sordid poverty it disguises runs through all the music-hall texts, a source of both humour and pathos. The "Great

Concubines of History" parading on stage during a long, unpaid rehearsal, suffer from "swollen feet and weak ankles" and "yawn themselves to death" (*CSC*, 145). Not yet in costume, the Marquise de Pompadour is dressed in "black knickers with bare knees showing above her black stockings" and in one of Colette's paradoxical analogies is said to "bear a strange resemblance to a young drummer boy of the Revolution" (*CSC*, 144–5). The analogy here, however, also indicates the central theme of the text, for the weary, penniless dancers are considering going on strike. Militancy is not their custom, for like the woman in the role of Madame de Montespan who "has more than enough on her hands looking after her man and two kids far out near Chateau-d'Eau district" (*CSC*, 145) they have domestic responsibilities, and anyway "If we strike, where will it get us? It will only help to fatten the cinema crowd" (*CSC*, 146). The strike does not happen this time either, but Colette establishes the conditions that would motivate industrial action and, as the socialist historian Dolleans acknowledged in a 1913 review, she produces a "forceful but restrained" exposure of the material conditions off-stage at the music-hall.[1]

* * *

Colette lived through two world wars and chronicled both in newspaper articles later edited in volume form. In World War I she was writing mainly for *Le Matin*, reporting on trips to the Front and to Italy as well as on life in wartime Paris, in a series of articles later published under the title *Les Heures longues* (*The Long Hours*, 1917). Texts written during and about World War II can be found in *Looking Backwards* (*Journal à rebours*, 1941) and in *The Evening Star* (*L'Etoile vesper*, 1946). Between 1939 and 1945 Colette wrote of the experience she shared with millions of her compatriots, that of an initial flight before the invading German army, then of the hard, daily reality of Occupation shot through with anxiety about her Jewish husband, Maurice Goudeket. These texts offer little reflection on the causes or the progress of the wars, but adopt the perspective of the civilian caught up in the disruption and the pain of wartime.

In the first text of *Les Heures longues* the news of the outbreak of war reaches a quiet seaside town in Brittany, and the tranquillity of sea and shore is replaced by the tumult of human anxiety, bells tolling, drums banging, shouts and the sounds of weeping. The world is turned upside down just as the sea "inverts the image of the purple rocks" (*HL*, 478). The suffering of war is neither minimised nor glorified. The wounded soldiers in the military hospital in 1914 have horrible injuries but retain a self-mocking sense of humour:

> the poor monster with his shattered purple head winks at me with his one remaining eye and says through his mischievous half a mouth: "You've got to admit I've got what they call a ruddy complexion!" (*HL*, 481)

Looking Backwards opens with the long procession of refugees struggling south in the exodus of 1940, and with a comparison between the writer's dogged return in times of disaster to "the same obligation, which is perhaps only a temptation: to write, to depict" and the stolid return of the peasant to his tilling after "the passage of armour-shielded invaders over (his) labour" (*LB*, 67). The moment in 1941 when German soldiers came to arrest Maurice and take him to a deportation camp is evoked with a quiet sense of horror and of "the perfect and classical nightmare of absence" (*ES*, 20). The emphasis, in both wars, is on the civilian's immediate concern with shared suffering and with survival.

What is most accentuated throughout these texts is the

human capacity for adapting, making and mending, what in *From My Window* (1942) Colette names *bricolage* or "making something out of nothing" (*LB*, 146). The trip to Verdun in 1914 reveals the practical courage of the population close to the Front: inventing dishes like "rice in milk without the milk" to overcome food shortages, finding entertainment in the air battles overhead, enjoying (in the case of those wives and lovers who like Colette had secretly joined their soldier husbands) the pleasure of a temporarily simple, cloistered life of love. Back in Paris women organise paid employment for wives suddenly bereft of income, old men enjoy learning to crochet and discovering "that women talk to each other, that they think, that they suffer gracefully . . . and what gaps there are in a masculine education!" (*HL*, 486).

In World War II Colette's neighbours in the Palais Royal adopt their own everyday forms of Resistance, finding ways "to mock, resist, evade, to slacken the torturing bonds, to thwart the spies" (*ES*, 24) by sheltering members of the Resistance, Jews and English parachutists, by refusing the elementary collaboration of a smile to the occupying soldiers. Faced with shortages the Parisians live "not just by restrictions, but by inventions and paradoxes" (*LB*, 137), scouring the flea-market for adaptable objects, buying monumental Second Empire wooden sculptures by the kilo as fuel: "Ah, if the Second Empire sculptor had had a taste for elephants, my winter would be assured" (*LB*, 191). One male friend of "Colette's", despairing of finding men's underwear for sale, proudly shows her the "ravishing little ladies knickers in pink cotton with a hem in sky blue machine-made lace" (*LB*, 192) he is now wearing.

The examples given are often, like this one, comic and apparently trivial but the attitudes they exemplify are both serious and consistent with those which underlie the literary texts. The virtues of resilience, flexibility of mind and humour are implicitly praised and are firmly linked to the importance of physical well-being as Colette, cheerfully adopting the role of advice columnist and Agony Aunt, advocates keeping warm in bed by "Leaving room for the cat" (*LB*, 132) and offers her readers cheap and substantial recipes. Conversely self-pity, inflated nationalism and moral censoriousness receive short shrift. In World War I Colette is to be read exhorting readers to have sympathy for the women who bore the illegitimate children of German soldiers (*HL*, 508–9): in her texts on World War II one of the most haunting figures is that of a French prostitute picked up and deported to work in Germany during the Occupation (*ES*, 33–4). The famous names of the wars, the heroes, simply do not appear.

Between 1907 and the 1920s one of the devices used by Colette to comment on contemporary society is the character "My Friend Valentine". Valentine is a fashionable young woman-about-town, with her respectable husband, her artist lover, her strict observation of the codes of elegant behaviour, her tastes and pleasures entirely determined by fashion rather than inclination. When the war comes for example, "like everyone else she knits, cries a little in secret, writes every day to her husband in the trenches".[2]

Valentine is recounted in the third person or addressed by letter in tones of affectionate exasperation, for her function is to establish a contrast between the free and easy lifestyle and libertarian morality of the narrator, and the restrictive, frequently hypocritical codes of the dominant class. Valentine is shocked by "Colette's" dancing almost nude on stage, but happily wears dresses that "outline her . . . worse than naked" and "comes out of the water at Trouville with nipples showing under (her) tight silk bathing suit glistening like a wet fish" (*CSC*, 47). She is horrified that "Colette" should frequent the ill-famed Semiramis bar with its "low-class crowd" of homosexuals and prostitutes which provides the occasion for a defence of the "grumpy motherliness" of its owner and of her gruff kindliness towards the thin little dancers from the music-hall and towards the young male homosexuals "gentle, weary, with their painted eyelids heavy with sleep" (*CSC*, 53). Valentine's "correct little person",[3] restricted physically by uncomfortable fashions, mentally by a profound conformism, allows Colette to offer a defence of a less orthodox morality and a benevolent though acute critique of contemporary values.

Valentine performs "with imbecilic fervour . . . the rites ordained by Fashion" (*CSC*, 60) and slavishly obeys her "despotic" master couturier whom the narrator sees as motivated by "the disgusted misogyny that comes from dealing with too many females, the pleasure he takes in making them ugly, in humiliating them . . ." (*CSC*, 74). Fashion is a regular theme of Colette's journalism, for it is partly through fashion that a society constructs its version of femininity and determines women's physical comfort and freedom. The texts on fashion are predominantly critical, emphasising the dangers to health and the constraints on mobility caused by corsets, high heels, tight skirts and other aspects of what a 1914 article terms fashion's "martyrology".

World War I appeared to herald an era of more comfortable female clothing, but Colette's articles insist that the imperative to be boyishly slender introduced its own constraints. The corset maker berates a silent "Colette" for having grown stout and for insisting on wearing only "little garter belts, which just leave you looking heavy and eccentric!", before extolling the virtues of her new invention for concealing unfashionable curves.

> Well, you grab hold of the breast, like this . . . and fold it, at the bottom, as you press it back as far as you can on the sides. Over that, you put a little brassière . . . (*CSC*, 37)

The female body becomes mere raw material, its parts optional accessories. The return of the breast is ironically hailed in a 1924 article:

> You thought they didn't exist any longer, that they were all over with, absolutely done for, their name ostracized, their amiable or indiscreet turgescence dead and deflated like a gold-beater's skin? . . . If you don't mind, Madame, lets bring things up to date. They exist, and persist, however criticized and persecuted they may be. (*JM*, 75–6)

The concern with the evolution and the implications of fashion, like the inclusion of recipes and the discussion of embroidery in Colette's late volumes, assumes a female readership. When Colette was sent to cover sensational criminal trails or to interview politicians her implied audience remained a predominantly female one, for her perspective was far from that of the conventional reporter. Rather than the gory details of the crime, or the legal and moral guilt of the criminal, Colette tends to focus on the defiant dignity and the stubborn resilience of the women involved. Madame Guillotin, whose lover was accused in 1912 of murdering her husband, and who was suspected of complicity in the crime, is a splendid figure as she gives evidence: "an embodiment of female courage. Once again I exclaim to myself 'What a solid creature a woman is!' "[4] The only woman accomplice in the anarchist Bonnot gang "needs no-one" in court. "Her aggressive innocence is quite unperturbed . . . I thought for a moment she was going to give the presiding judge 500 lines!"[5]

The reports invariably adopt an unconventional perspective that decentres familiar categories of guilt and innocence: Marie Becker, accused of poisoning the old people she nursed, was also "caring for their loneliness" and was as generous with "kisses on the hands" as with her poison. "And it has not been proved that loneliness has no need of digitalin."[6] Oum-el-Hassen, a Moroccan brothel keeper loyal to the French, who tortured and killed her young charges, is not exonerated by Colette's account but is seen as alien to the values in whose name she is condemned, having known only "domination, the camaraderie of the camps, a certain type of violence which she thought venial, and a personal ideal of love" (*LB*, 40). A series of articles on the country's great men[7] undermine their own explicitly respectful tone by concentrating, exclusively and in detail, on the physical appearance of the politicians interviewed.

Colette's individual and, in the precise meaning of the word, eccentric commentaries on society appeared daily in *Le Matin* from 1911 to 1924, in her column "Tales of a Thousand and One Nights", and thereafter in other major French daily papers. There was another facet, too, to her public involvement in contemporary culture in that Colette was an enthusiastic film and theatre goer, and apart from producing (with Leopold Marchand) stage adaptations of some of her novels, and writing sub-titles and screenplays for a small number of films,[8] she worked as a film critic in the days of the silent movies and was the weekly drama critic for *Le Journal* in the 1930s.

As a critic in the early days of commercial cinema Colette was quick to identify the specifically visual language of the new medium, highlighting the quality of the image and of frame composition as well as that of acting and narrative. Abel Gance's *Mater Dolorosa* (1917) is praised for its "unusually rich lighting, gold-tinted whites and deep, rich blacks . . . and certain dark shots in which the pleading face of Mme Emmy Lynn floats like a decapitated flower" (*CC*, 47). Intolerant of platitudes, Colette delighted in identifying and making fun of the clichés of cinema narrative, publishing, for example, a tongue in cheek catechism for the aspiring scriptwriter in 1918:

> *Q*. What are the occupations of an evil woman, once she is alone on the screen?
> *A*. She lights a cigarette and lies on a couch . . .
> *Q*. What, at the end of a sensational film, is the fate of the *femme fatale*?
> *A*. She dies, preferably on three steps covered by a rug . . .[9]

Colette also condemns the stereotyped romantic plot with its strong, masterful hero and "frail, blonde, etcetera" heroine (*CC*, 63), appreciating conversely the audacious toughness of Mae West and lamenting the star's loss of weight in later films. Her solid, curvaceous body, for Colette, was central to the persona she created, "signifying . . . sensuality and brutality" (*CC*, 275).

In the theatre, Colette's range of tastes and interests is wide. At one end of the spectrum lie her appreciative reviews of the *Folies-Bergère* shows, where again she defends the beauty of a plump female body against the fashionable slenderness of the 1930s and with a self-mocking nod at her own, now generous build, insists on the need for an adequate diet for reasons of both health and pleasure. The reviews also extend though to "serious" theatre, and just as she insists on the specifically visual qualities of film as a medium so Colette emphasises the success or failure of plays as spectacle rather than as expression of ideas or values.

The play *The Leader* by Drieu la Rochelle, a fascist sympathiser, is criticised as a theatrical failure: "Since a play is not a plebiscite, I object to Drieu's using the stage only to ask us questions . . .",[10] whereas the Pitoeff's production of Ibsen's *The Wild Duck* in 1934 is praised for its spectacular fusion of genres, the tragic and the comic.[11]

The implicit criteria here – the dislike of didacticism and of rigid systems of thought, the preference for plurality and paradox – are consistent with the values that underlie the whole of Colette's textual production.

* * *

It is one thing to demonstrate that through her journalism Colette participated in the social and cultural life of her society, quite another to claim a social and even a political dimension for literary works which have generally been perceived as apolitical, and as restricted to the domestic and emotional sphere. "Colette" said Simone de Beauvoir, "is really very taken up with her little stories about love, housework, the washing and animals."[12] In terms of Sartrian commitment Colette certainly appears lacking: despite her involvement in a political milieu through Henri de Jouvenel and her long career as a journalist, despite living through an era that saw two world wars, the rise of Fascism, the Spanish Civil War, and the internal political upheavals of the 1930s, there is very little reference in Colette's literary works to national or international political events. However, the absence of specific reference to historical events does not prevent her texts from being read as "an expression, through the mediation of writing, of an experience of the social order".[13] Colette's fiction represents a female experience of the patriarchal social order of early twentieth-century France, and read from this perspective reveals a substantial degree of social, and ultimately of economic, realism.

The transition from girlhood to womanhood is invariably represented in Colette's texts as a fall or a decline. Her heroines' experience of a radical discontinuity between childhood identity and adult femininity comes close to Beauvoir's analysis of female adolescence in *The Second Sex* (*Le Deuxième sexe*, 1949).

> . . . a conflict breaks out between her original claim to be subject, active, free, and, on the other hand, her erotic urges and the social pressure to accept herself as passive object. Her spontaneous tendency is to regard herself as the essential: how can she make up her mind to become the inessential? (*SS*, 360)

Thus "Colette", addressing her fictional double Claudine in the short text "The Mirror", defines the process of becoming a woman as a loss of self-esteem and a curtailment of scope:

> But what I have lost, Claudine, is my fine pride, the secret certainty that I was a precious child, the sense of possessing within me the extraordinary spirit of an intelligent man and a woman in love . . . Alas, I lost all that to become, after all, just a woman . . . (*VV*, 1032)

As Renée, on tour, passes through the region of her childhood she evokes the "tall child" with "regal plaits" she used to be, and in a letter to Max expresses the fear that what he loves in her may be the mere disguise of womanhood:

> . . . Are not the things you love in me the things which change me and deceive you, my curls clustering thick as leaves, my eyes which the blue kohl lengthens and suffuses, the artificial smoothness of my powdered skin? (*V*, 149)

Vinca (*Ripening Seed*), is situated at the juncture between child and adult identity, half little girl with her tucked-up skirts and passion for shrimping, half grown-up with her graceful limbs and her quick understanding of Phil's desire for the "Lady in white". In this dual characterisation dignity is a quality of childhood and Vinca's more "womanly" words and gestures are associated with humiliation: though she is frequently tougher and more aggressive than Phil, whenever the potentially sexual dimension of their relationship is acknowledged Vinca "fight(s) against the precocious, overpowering instinct to give all" (*RS*, 6), is "beset beyond her years by the awkwardness, the self-abasement . . . of someone really in love" (*RS*, 3), accepts her adult fate "submissively" (*RS*, 19) and receives Phil's criticism of her untidy hair with "a humble appeal . . . (in) her eyes" (*RS*, 16).

This is not because Colette perceives being a woman as a state of inherent humiliation. It is because heterosexual love in these texts does not occur in a vacuum: it is lived within specific material and social conditions. Women do not choose marriage or cohabitation out of mere inclination: it is also their principal means of economic survival. When Renée, the "Vagabond", divorces Taillandy, she immediately loses her place in the class structure and ceases to be accepted in her husband's cultured bourgeois milieu. She also confronts the problem of earning a living as a woman educated only for marriage: ". . . what would you have me do? Sewing, or typing, or street-walking?" (*V*, 122). Renee's solution, like Colette's, is the music-hall, "the job of those who never learnt one", but, like the other female professions listed here, performing on the stage is a low paid and a low status job.

Bastienne and Mitsou, like many of their sisters, survive by accepting the support of older lovers; the sisters of *The Toutounier* (1939), who also tried to make a living in the performing arts, all face "the worst of women's tasks, making sure of a man" (*T*, 183) and the temptation to do like their youngest Bizoute, who "absentmindedly got married . . . (on) a day when the cupboard was particularly bare" (*T*, 137). The poverty of the single woman encourages her to exchange her freedom for security and comfort:

thus Renée is briefly tempted by the prospect of marriage to Max, and Julie de Carneilhan only prevents herself from accepting gifts from Coco Vatard by reflecting that "if this blessed innocent gives me some of his salary and then thinks I'm in his debt, life will again be a hell" (*JC*, 126).

Relationships are not, of course, mere financial transactions in Colette's fiction, and love and desire are central to the characters' motivation. But marriage and what the French call *concubinage* – in the milieu of Colette's narratives the distinction is not always crucial – are seen as institutions, with their own determining rites and structures of power. Economic power is, on the whole, invested in the male partner: even where the wife or mistress has means of her own, the couple's place of residence belongs to the man (for example in *The Captive*, *Chéri*, *The Cat*) and the main source of income is his, but this financial control then extends to an assumption of overall authority. It is not only those characters who are assertive and dominant as individuals, like Taillandy (*The Vagabond*), Farou (*The Other One*) and d'Espivant (*Julie de Carneilhan*) who assume the role of master, but also characters who are, in other respects, gentle and sensitive lovers. Alice is happy with Michel until jealousy recasts him as the proprietorial husband and he follows the logic of his role as far as death: "an actor, a third-rate actor, like all men" (*Duo*, 34) rages Alice. The alliance that forms between Alice and the maid Maria, reinforces the idea that marriage institutionalises male authority. Maria's man is personally unimpressive, but as a husband he is dominant to the point of violence; Maria admits to Alice that he inflicted the burn on her arm.

"Your husband? What's got into him?"
"He's having his revenge."
"What for?"
"For the fact that he's my husband and I'm his wife.

> That's quite enough. Doesn't Madame agree?" (*Duo*, 109)

Chéri reveals a vulnerable, androgynous identity in his relationship with Léa, but in marriage to Edmée attempts to take on the behaviour of a husband.

> "Oh! she won't be allowed to have a say in anything," Chéri declared. "She's going to be my wife, isn't she? Let her kiss the sacred ground I tread on, and thank her lucky stars for the privilege." (*C*, 45)

Renée defines the role of wife as that of "mediator . . . between Monsieur and the rest of humanity . . . Steward, sick-nurse, children's nurse . . ." (*V*, 126), and Gigi's promotion from prospective mistress to wife, in what is usually interpreted as the happy ending of her story, is marked by her sadness rather than by joy.

Marriage or *concubinage* are often material necessities for women in Colette's world, but they are also forms of social organisation founded on male authority and this meaning surfaces whatever the individual personalities of the couple concerned. A woman's economic independence thus becomes an important precondition of her freedom and Renée, despite her straitened circumstances, rejoices in "bartering my gestures, my dances, and the sound of my voice for hard cash . . . On my good days I joyfully say over and over again to myself that I earn my living" (*V*, 24).

Léa, one of Colette's strongest female characters, has made a fortune by strategic use of her greatest asset in her career as a successful courtesan. If she can live, in her maturity, according to a different economy that demands no system of exchange with Chéri but simply gives in abundance, it is because she has managed to negotiate the dominant system and emerge with her independence. The coolly autonomous Edmée of *The Last of Chéri* has significantly taken over the financial management of their joint affairs and reversed the relationship assumed by law and by conventional practice. The "Colette" of *Chance Acquaintances* (*Chambre d'hotel*, 1940), "Bella Vista", "Rainy Moon" or *Break of Day*, a mobile, curious, vital narrator has the precarious but real financial autonomy of the professional writer.

Colette's narratives do, in fact, take place in a world that has a clear economic dimension. Wealth is owned and controlled by men of the middle and upper classes; women may gain access to wealth by forming sexual alliances with men or, failing this, by selling their labour, on the whole, since their education has given them few skills at low prices. Few of the stories and novels are very specifically dated; they tend, rather to represent what was broadly the situation of women in France throughout the first half of the twentieth century. French women were only granted the vote, and hence legal recognition as citizens of France in 1944, and though a law passed in 1938 permitted them for the first time to open a bank account or apply for a passport without the authority of a husband, the latter could still refuse his wife the right to work outside the home.[14] There is, however, a more precise historical focus in some of the novels, for the 1914–18 war appears in Colette's work as a pivotal event which modified, if not the real distribution of power, at least the behaviour demanded of men and women.

The First World War mobilised the vast majority of French men between the ages of twenty and sixty-five and killed ten per cent of them. In the absence of the soldiers, women were obliged to take over not only new kinds of work, but also legal and financial responsibilities, and despite a highly successful "Back to the Home" campaign once the men were demobilised, this temporary emancipation produced a visible change in female dress and behaviour after the war, a move away from traditionally female sectors of employment such as domestic labour towards clerical and secretarial work, and a renewed, if unsuccessful, campaign for the vote. Many men felt resentful and alienated at this apparent challenge to their supremacy, a reaction apparent, for example, in the lampooning of the "New Woman", in the Press of the 1920s. *Le Figaro* warned women to "Beware! The bearded woman and the armoured woman have less power over us than a lovely, frail girl of twenty",[15] and *Le Progrès Civique* berated "this generation of bony women with their shaven napes, their awkward manners . . . and their dogma of non-maternity!".[16] At the same time the war had determined certain changes in the economy, replacing the pre-war emphasis on a stable currency and on consumption, with a new drive for productivity and industrialisation. "Industry was fashionable and considered necessary to France's greatness".[17]

This social climate is clearly present in Colette's fiction for the novels of the 1920s and early 1930s, from *Chéri* to *Duo*, foreground the problem of masculine identity in the face of female autonomy, and replace the wealthy, idle heroes of the earlier fiction with men who work for a living. If Max Dufferein-Chautel (*The Vagabond*) could live happily on his unearned income from the parental saw-mills, Alain of *The Cat*, like most of the other heroes of Colette's post-war fiction, must work in his father's firm, and Chéri feels out of place and superfluous in the new world of industrious profiteering:

> Before the war I was rich, damn it! . . . But now it's not at all the same thing. People have got the jitters. And work, and activity, and duty . . . Is it really wrong to be rich, and take life easy? (*LC*, 157)

Chéri's sense of alienation focuses particularly on the

person of his wife, Edmée. Focalised almost entirely through Chéri's eyes, Edmée represents male fears of the emancipated woman, for Chéri's response to her thorough efficiency is to ask "but where do I come in?" (*LC*, 147), and his sense of no longer possessing a role in life is one of the factors which lead to his suicide. Edmée is cold, brisk and callous partly because she is the embodiment of male anxiety, just as in *The Cat* Camille's command of the idiom of commerce ("Business going all right? Crisis still expected? Have you managed to put over the spotted *foulard* on the big dress-houses?" [*Cat*, 93]) and her liking for the signs of modernity such as fast cars and high-rise flats, are seen from the anxious, hostile perspective of Alain.

But these ambivalent female characters, admirably independent yet identified with the harshest face of modernity, represent more than just the spectres of male fear. Firstly, the contrast between their vigorous, competent adaptation to a changed social world and their husbands' desperate retreat into the past demonstrates the absurdity of institutionalised gender roles, with their blindness to the qualities of the individual. Secondly, and more subtly, Edmée and Camille should perhaps also be read as admonitory figures who warn of the dangers of mere emancipation, of emulating men rather than questioning those values identified with "the masculine". Edmée, like her mother-in-law, becomes an efficient and ruthless business woman, rising to fame and fortune through her work for wounded soldiers and profiteering thanks to political connections. Camille's attack on Saha is disturbingly consistent with her whole pragmatic, materialist approach to life. The pursuit of independence, the determination to control one's own destiny, are worthy female goals in Colette's fiction, but they can not be equated with a wholesale adoption of masculine values.

As a journalist and as a writer of fiction Colette's perspective on her society is personal and experiential: the texts focus on individuals rather than on collectivities and on the everyday rather than the exceptional. She writes, to echo again one of her own titles, from within the crowd, particularly if we imagine the crowd as a female crowd. Though as a woman she took little interest in politics or in feminism as a movement, this is immaterial to her work as a writer, for within the texts the personal is political. When Colette describes the poverty and the solidarity of her companions in the music-hall, when she presents a prostitute as her example of resilience under the Occupation, or humorously exposes the harmful effects of the corset, or situates love in a material context of economic power – then the personal and the political are inseparable. Colette may have written about love, but her writing is more appropriately seen in terms of realism than of romance.

5 The Body in the Text

Colette's fictional world is primarily a physical, sensual place. The production of identifiable characters and of the conflicts which generate plot depends less on contrasts of personality and beliefs than on differences of colour, form and smell. The most famous of the fictional texts can be resumed or recalled in terms of a sharply visual image: Chéri's beauty etched against the warm pink of Léa; slow, dark Fanny and silvery-yellow Jane in *The Other One*; the trio of blonde Alain, dark Camille and many-hued Saha in *The Cat*. It is not simply that character is expressed through physical appearance, a device much used in realist fiction, but that identity itself is produced by the body, both within the text and in the world to which it refers.

Chéri is granted some minimal biography, and a particular emotional situation, but since he is given as incapable of introspection or articulation of feeling, it is his body that functions as primary signifier of the character. In this Chéri is typical of Colette's characters: the technique whereby characters are produced in the text obviates any distinction between physical and "inner" identity, and the primacy accorded to the body in the construction of identity is reflected, sometimes humorously, in the narratives where personality and even name may be determined by appearance. Chéri, Léa reflects, might have "turned into a decent sort, perhaps, if he'd only had pink chaps like a pork-butcher and flat feet" (*C*, 101); Albin Chaveriat in "The Tender Shoot" is addressed as "Colonel" not because he has ever held military rank but because he has a brush of white hair, a moustache and a limp (*CSC*,

422); Gigi's grandmother comes to be called Inez because she has developed Spanish colouring and features (*G*, 9).

The concept of an inner identity separable from and superior to the body is fundamental to Western thought. Not only does Christianity situate the true, transcendent self as merely lodging in the body on a temporary basis, but secular, rationalist thought also tends to centre identity in the brain and relegate the body to secondary status: "I think, therefore I am". French culture in particular is permeated with the Cartesian emphasis on the intellect, so that even Simone de Beauvoir in her radical *Second Sex* sees the origins of women's oppression in their enslavement to a merely physical reality of reproduction and menstrual cycle, and their potential liberation as a rational project of transcendence. In this sense the indivisibility of body and self in Colette's writing is transgressive, and partially explains why she was relegated for a long time, to a second division of not fully serious writers, charged with being "unintellectual and immodest",[1] with "reduc(ing) human beings to their instincts alone".[2] The central place accorded to the body, as well as a certain serene impiety in the manner of its representation, account for the critics' indignation.

The body, then, is not just described to establish character in Colette's texts but functions constantly as a multiple and detailed signifier. Each character is constructed by a certain number of physical features, some of which signify by reference to a fixed and familiar code of meaning: Farou of *The Other One* is tall, broad and robust in a way that at once connotes confident masculinity; Vinca of *Ripening Seed* is long-legged, gawky and graceful at the turning point between childhood and womanhood. Certain colours also function through a system of standardised connotations: Léa's predominant pink, that extends from body to clothing and possessions, signifies above all warmth and femininity, whilst her blue eyes connote her lucidity and strength of spirit. Edmée's transition from a predominant hazel in *Chéri* to white in *The Last of Chéri*, clearly translates her development from tentative immaturity to crisp, decisive independence. The "blue lieutenant" of *Mitsou* is coloured the blue of Mitsou's dreams, with the edge of sadness that the colour also connotes, and the strongly contrasting tones of the dark, red-lipped Camille in *The Cat* represent her robust confidence.

Other bodily signifiers depend less on an established code than on a system established within the texts themselves. Certain smells repeatedly connote desirable masculinity: Farou's hands smell of "dark skin, tobacco and scented lotion" (*OO*, 65), just as the smell of "leather, toilet water, tobacco and printer's ink" (*T*, 64) evokes the dead Michel for Alice. Renée in *The Captive* notices the slightly burnt smell of her lover's hair, the same smell as that of Vial in *Break of Day*. A change of body smell communicates an emotion or thought more precisely than words, so that Michel can discover his wife's infidelity through her physical anxiety:

> his nostrils detected the scent that revealed emotion, sweat dragged cruelly out of the pores by fear, by anguish, the scent which caricatured the perfume of sandalwood, of heated boxwood, the perfume reserved for the hours of love . . . (*Duo*, 16)

and dogs and cats detect the scent of unhappy love at once on their owners, disliking and fleeing the smell of defeat. For love itself is experienced as a change of physical state, generally one close to sickness. Léa believes she is ill until she realises that the fever and nausea she feels are her hitherto unrecognised love for Chéri. Once Gaston Lachaille falls in love with Gigi he becomes "haggard, his eyes bloodshot" (*G*, 56), whilst Gigi becomes feverish. Marco in "The Kepi" gets fat on love, but it is an excessive gain of weight that makes her age rapidly and develop what the narrator terms "a behind like a cobbler's" and "breasts like jellyfish, very broad and decidedly flabby" (*CSC*, 522). Thus emotion, in this case quite literally, becomes flesh.

The texts' internal codification of physical features is most original in the selection of and the precision of detail. Eyes are not only of a predominant colour, they are "elongated like leaves, with their mingled green and grey, pale in the evening by lamplight, darker in the morning" (*Duo*, 16), or have a "smoky tone on (the) eyelids" with "a double row of stiff, thick eyelashes" (*V*, 97). Eyes are conventional signifiers of thought and feeling, noses less so, but in Colette's writing noses, nostrils and other less probable features also function to create character: Jean's health and seductiveness are indicated by his "beautiful pale nostrils unspoilt by redness or blackheads, whose wings were welded to the face by a deep, well-chiselled groove" (*Cap*, 67), whilst Gérard Haume in *Chance Acquaintances* displays a tense, furtive disposition by a "lean nose with the skin stretched almost transparently over the bridge" (*CA*, 24). Fanny's dark passivity gives her rather bovine "soft, velvety nostrils" (*OO*, 46) in contrast to Julie de Carneilhan whose nostrils when contracted accentuate "the 'wild animal' side of her character" (*JC*, 9) and whose resolute, ready for anything mood is signified by her "nostrils particularly open to the wind" (*JC*, 163).

Necks indicate sensuality: Jean runs his finger between collar and Adam's apple to draw attention to his "very youthful neck" (*Cap*, 74), or they signify physical and moral strength as in the case of Madame Haume's "firm, thick neck – a smooth column instinct with exceptional power" (*CA*, 23) or Gigi's "lovely strong neck" (*G*, 39). The joints of the body, and particularly knees, are worthy of attention and at their best indicate an elegance or sensitivity that is not only physical: Gigi's knee-caps are a "perfect oval shape" (*G*, 7) and Vinca's knees form a "delicate oval beneath their hard exterior" (*RS*, 63); knees like Chéri's, Léa muses, "you don't find running about the streets every day of the week" (*C*, 39), for they are as exceptional as the statuesque way his neck joins his shoulders.

The focaliser in these instances of detailed physical description may be an extradiegetic narrator (i.e. one external to the story she/he narrates) or one character observing another. In the latter case the degree of detail tends to signify the intensity of the watcher's gaze, and often therefore to connote love or desire. When Renée notices that Max's dark eyes in fact "beneath all that black . . . are a tawny grey" (*V*, 66), or when only Léa sees that Chéri's eyes "looked black, but their true shade . . . was a dark almost reddish brown" (*C*, 46), or when the "blue lieutenant" explains to Mitsou how he remembers that "because of the petunia red of your cheeks, under the harsh light your arms and the furrow of your back looked green, green like the white lilacs that are forced to bloom in winter" (*M*, 683), their close attention indicates their emotion.

Fanny intones a litany of praise to the colour of Farou's eyes: "Colour of old amber . . . colour of angry gold . . . of burning topaz . . . of the Moret nuns' barleysugar" (*OO*, 52) whereas the narrator of *Break of Day* appreciative but undesiring, notes Vial's "clear-cut, alert, expressive body" (*BD*, 59) but finds the lines of his face only "rather sleepy". "I haven't omitted to point out to Vial" she adds "that he might be guillotined without anyone's noticing."

Dramas are constructed, on one level, around physical contrast or change. Several of the fictional texts establish the difference and potential conflict between characters by a contrast of colouring: Vinca's blue eyes and corn-coloured hair link her to the natural world as surely as Madame Dalleray's white and vivid reds and gold connect her to an urban sophisticated culture; Chéri's white skin and dark hair contrast in their stark immobility both with the vibrant pink and blue of Léa and with the subtle, changing tones of Edmée. The potential, and unrealised, conflict between the wife and the "other woman" which is at the centre of *The Other One* is established by the women's physical difference: Fanny is rounded, slow-moving, dark with "prominent, gentle eyes and full, rounded mouth" (*OO*, 8). Jane is slim, active and fair "if 'fair' can be applied to the colour of fine ash" (*OO*, 8).

This presence of opposing colours is repeated in *The Cat*, where the conflict between Alain and Camille is visible at once in their radically different colouring, she dark to an extent that scandalises Alain who observes the:

> short hairs on her shaved neck, ranged like the prickles of a sea-urchin . . . the shortest of them were blue and visible under the fine skin before each one emerged through a small blackened pore (*Cat*, 109)

he blond to the extent that Camille cries "It's crazy to be as fair as all that!" (*Cat*, 64). And in the short stories, which often depend for their impact on the rapid establishment of a central tension or conflict, physical contrast is frequently crucial to the narrative. "The Other Wife" ("L'Autre femme") brings together the ex-wife, with her smooth, shiny hair and the "dusky and ample" Alice (*CSC*, 264); "The Portrait" ("Le Portrait") opposes the elegant, bony, dark Alice to the plump, blonde Lily, and in "Rainy Moon" one of the central narrative tensions is formed by the contrast between the two sisters, one frail, fair and blue-eyed and the other black-haired with a "short, slightly Spanish figure" (*CSC*, 372).

In two splendidly precise critical studies published in France in the early 1970s, Marcelle Biolley-Godino and Yannick Resch examined Colette's representation of the body in terms of gender: Biolley-Godino with an analysis of male characters in Colette's fiction *L'Homme-Objet chez Colette* (*Man as object in Colette's work*) and Resch with a study of the textualisation of the female body *Corps feminin, corps textuel* (*Female body/Textual body*). Though the primacy of the body in the construction of character and narrative is itself an original aspect of Colette's writing, it is from the perspective of gender that her radicalism becomes most apparent, and that the reader meets what Biolley-Godino terms "a veritable revolution" in the way the male and female body are viewed.

A convention deeply rooted in patriarchal culture differentiates between the significance of beauty in men and in women: as the primary subject of vision and as the active agent of desire, the male body is less visible, less defined in terms of beauty than the female body, which is essentially an object of vision, an object of desire. In the novel this tends to produce representations of the male body which are transparently metaphorical: the text invites the reader to pass straight through the denotative level that names physical features to a connotative level that indicates attributes of character. A good example of this familiar convention can be found in the novels of Marcelle Tinayre, Colette's contemporary and seen by critics of her time very much as a women's novelist who represented a feminine view of the world. In the 1908 novel *Avant l'amour* (*Before Love*), a novel that quite explicitly defends women's right to sexual desire, Tinayre describes her hero thus:

> He was interesting because of the fire of intelligence that burnt in his gold eyes . . . vigorous and hard, with nothing common in his appearance. (*AA*, 41)

Elsewhere he has a:

dark moustache, shadowing his fine, hard mouth. A clear-cut, rounded, Roman chin, hollow cheeks, hard onyx eyes that revealed intelligence and obstinacy. (*AA*, 10)

The hero of Tinayre's *La Rebelle* (1905) has a "clear, sharp, cool gaze" and "steel grey eyes" (*R*, 137). These descriptions produce only a general image of the hero's appearance, but they immediately indicate moral and psychological qualities: intelligence, strength of mind, a potential for passion. Descriptions of the heroine differ in the extent and nature of the physical detail provided: since in *Avant l'amour* the heroine is also the narrator, it is through the device of the mirror that a physical description can be afforded, and it is as she observes her reflection that Marianne describes "a girl neither very pretty nor ugly either, quite well built for her 17 years, with a well-rounded bosom . . ." (*AA*, 20).

In *La Rebelle* the difference in physical characterisation is even more marked, for despite the fact that the "rebel" Josyane is the novel's central character and focaliser for most of the novel, Tinayre regularly transfers focalisation to the hero or to an unnamed male observer in order to establish her heroine's sexual beauty. She is introduced to the reader walking down a Parisian street with her dress of soft material drawn tight over her "pretty waist and hips" (*R*, 1) and later, in the lovemaking scenes, it is Josyane's "swelling bosom" and "matte white flesh" (*R*, 235) that appear in the text, not the body of her lover. In this Tinayre merely observes much the same practice as the majority of her contemporaries and indeed of the mainstream novel today.

We have already seen that Colette's textualisation of bodies of both genders is too precise and complex to function as a transparent signifier for more abstract qualities, and this is the first sense in which her way of representing the male body is innovatory. As readers, our physical image of a Colette hero is not limited to his size and colouring but may extend to the shape of his nostrils, knees and neck, the precise shading of skin and hair on different parts of his body, his characteristic smell and whether or not he is eating well. Colette's second innovation though, which is very closely bound up with the first, is her introduction of a perspective of potential or actual desire. Male bodies in Colette's texts are defined and evaluated in terms of their sensuality and their erotic potential, sometimes quite seriously and sometimes in a way that is surely a tongue-in-cheek reversal of the norm. As Biolley-Godino puts it, in appropriately Mae Westian style, "You can love a man for his soul or his pectoral muscles. Colette opts for the muscles" (*L'Homme objet*, 32).

The focus of desire is frequently the mouth. Renée watches Jean, her friend's lover and later in the novel to become her own:

> But a yawn from Jean, May's Jean, suddenly interested me in this masculine face. I had never noticed before how the clean-shaved, sulky mouth, full-lipped but chiselled at the corners, revealed both the weaknesses and charms of his character – nor that the chin was at once obstinate and feminine, nor that the neck showing above the low collar was strong but so smoothly rounded that no muscles were visible. (*Cap*, 17)

Camille watches Alain drinking and is seized with "a sudden pang of desire: at the sight of his mouth pressing against the rim of the glass" (*Cat*, 62). The narrator of *Mitsou* dismisses Mitsou's own limited ability to appreciate the beauty of her Blue Lieutenant: having experience only of her middle-aged lover, "Mitsou called any man who didn't have a paunch well made" (*M*, 703) but the narrator details the sensuous pleasure of his mouth: "It was the first time that Mitsou had tasted, one after another, those smooth lips, that bold tongue and those small, closely set teeth" (*M*, 698). Alice remembers a brief but intensely erotic encounter with:

> the subtle man from Nice whose black hair shone like a bird's plumage. The colour of his lips was attractive, barely red, rather a pinkish beige . . . He had beautiful gums that framed the top of his teeth like tiny pink arcades . . . and plenty of other merits . . . (*Duo*, 102)

The "other merits" most frequently evoked are eyes, muscles and skill as a lover. Eyes are perceived less in terms of expression than of colour and form, like Michel's "tobacco-coloured" eyes (*Duo*, 7) or Gérard Haume's "slate-blue eyes, deeply set in bistred sockets" (*CA*, 24). Muscles become a focal point in *The Captive* when Renée watches Jean walking down to the sea "gentle and half-naked like a faun" and admires the way "his step sent rippling shadows over his back and that magnificent muscular V that one sees in beautiful statues" (*Cap*, 130) and in *Break of Day* when the narrator observes Vial's "beautifully muscled shoulders rising and falling like a bosom breathing" (*BD*, 38). The capacity for making love well is celebrated, for example, in Max when Renée, with a rare apology for her frankness, praises in him the

> subtle lover, born for women, and so skilled at divining that his caresses seem to know the thoughts behind my desire. He makes me think – and I blush for it – of the saying of a lascivious little music-hall comrade who boasted of the cleverness of a new lover: "My dear, one couldn't do better oneself!" (*V*,112)

These female characters who *see* men in sensual terms are not, within the text, consciously transgressing the rules but are simply behaving "naturally". That their perspective is to be read as the norm is confirmed by the supporting presence of a female chorus of minor characters. Léa's precise and epicurean appreciation of her young lover is echoed in the reaction of three errand girls to his appearance in the street: "Lawks! he's too good to be true! Let's touch him to see if he's real!" (*C*, 21). Petite-Chose, Mitsou's music-hall companion, enters Mitsou's dressing room, and the novel, with two young soldiers in tow and the words "Hide them for me, Mitsou ... they're so pretty!" (*M*, 651) and later describes the temptations of wartime when the streets are full of "gorgeous young soldiers all ... dressed up to attract attention. And we're supposed to keep our hands off!" she exclaims, incredulous and indignant (*M*, 672). In *The Last of Chéri* Léa's visitor Valerie, coolly dissects the qualities of a friend's new lover:

> Oh, my dear, what a disappointment! Tall, yes ... Eyes, yes, eyes, I've got nothing to say against the eyes. But ... something about the cheeks which is too rounded, too soft, and the ears set too low ... And holding himself as stiff as a poker. (*LC*, 185)

Valerie's critical detachment demonstrates that the male body may also be tried and found wanting as an object of desire. Chéri, the unwilling audience of this speech and of Léa's equally dispassionate reply, compares the women to "judges of pedigree fat cattle" (*LC*, 186). His resentment of their tone is justified, for this negative appraisal reveals very clearly how the objectification of the body can represent an attack, a deliberately deflating reduction of man to a set of physical attributes. And it is often as a response to men's sexual complacency, or as an act of self-defence, that this tactic is used. In the passage quoted here, Léa has successfully constructed a new identity in old age, but is made suddenly vulnerable by the unexpected arrival of her ex-lover: Valerie functions as an extension of Léa's defensively displayed detachment. Julie de Carneilhan, still tied by desire to her ex-husband, is accused of having an affair with his teenage step-son and defends the quality of her sexual tastes in a way that also serves to outrage Herbert:

> I agree he's very beautiful. But pff! you ought to know unless you've quite forgotten what I think of the Italian statuette kind of beauty. I bet he's got two lilac-coloured buttons on his chest and a dismal little ... "That's enough!" Espivant said. (*JC*, 144)

just as Léa deflates the aging Colonel Ypoustegue because he complacently assumes that she will have him.

> Léa, caught in his sudden kiss, had subjected him to the searching formidable gaze of the woman who knows exactly where to find the tell-tale marks of age. From the dried up, well cared for hands, ribbed with veins and tendons, her glance rose to the pouched chin and furrowed brows, returning cruelly to the mouth entrapped between double lines of inverted commas. (*C*, 99)

In "The Tender Shoot" the verbal attack comes as a response to Chaveriat's near seduction of Louise: her mother points out the signs of his age and inappropriateness as a lover for her daughter: "You see what he's got on his temples? White hairs, Louise ... and those wrinkles he's got under his eyes!" (*CSC*, 445)

The emphasis on the body in the construction of male characters, and the perspective of actual or potential desire, produce the originality of Colette's heroes and the lack of "masculinity" to which male critics like Henri Peyre and Jean Larnac have objected. "Can they really be called men?" asked Larnac, "these creatures distinguished only by their physical appearance and their way of making love?"[3] If Colette's heroes were felt to be "not proper men", though, this was surely also because of the terms in which they are described.

In Colette's writing the most sexually attractive men do not carry the distinguishing marks of heroic masculinity – strength, toughness, initiative – but have many features more commonly interpreted as feminine. The virile hero, whose attraction lies precisely in his otherness, is not entirely absent: he is there in Chéri's "hard, darkish chest, curved like a shield" (*C*, 15), in Jean's "silver eyes gleaming with a slightly negroid ferocity" (*Cap*, 90), and in Phil's upper lip "each day becoming more darkly shadowed" (*RS*, 84) to which Camille Dalleray's glance keeps returning. But those heroes who display only signs of the masculine tend to be resistible.

Max, the rejected suitor of *The Vagabond* is tall, dark and handsome so that he resembles "an amorous woodcutter" (*V*, 99); with the one exception of his long eyelashes he has a face "whose fault is excess of virility" (*V*, 104). In *The Last of Chéri* Edmée's "healthy, red-haired" doctor with his "thick, gentle hands" (*LC*, 212) represents competent and dependable masculinity as a foil to Chéri's withdrawal from the masculine role, but the novel's sympathies are so clearly with Chéri that this robust virility is a negative sign. The doctor's red hair also links him to the husband in the short story "The Hand" ("Le Main", 1924), which centres on the revulsion of a young wife as she contemplates the large, bestial hand of her sleeping husband with its "battle dress" of red hairs and its "powerful knuckles" (*CSC*, 247). The only male character who is virile in the most conventional way yet remains the object of the heroine's desire is Farou in *The Other One*, a novel that deals thematically with the power and attraction of the successful patriarch, and with female strategies of resistance. Farou is six feet tall, "tired but robust, ugly, perhaps, but certain of his charm" (*OO*, 29), and significantly leonine in colouring.

With this single exception, those of Colette's heroes who are most seductive display signs of the feminine. Jean of *The Captive* has a chin that is "obstinate and feminine" (*Cap*, 17), "feminine lips" and a "flawlessly smooth neck" (*Cap*, 94). Chéri has "tapering fingers that droop as he sleeps like wilting flowers: a hand not strictly feminine, yet a trifle prettier than one could have wished" (*C*, 22), and a body that is set off well by a string of pinkish pearls. Phil in *Ripening Seed* has the ambiguity of gender of the adolescent, Julie de Carneilhan's Herbert has feminine features. The traditional attributes of femininity become a component of male sexual attraction, as in the *Claudine* novels where the intensely feminine Marcel had already tempted both Annie and Claudine herself.

Lovers are drawn to each other not only by desire for what is opposite and separate, but also by their similarity, so that in *Mitsou*, for example, the initial attraction between the Blue Lieutenant and Mitsou herself is partly based on their likeness. As they look in the mirror they see "their two young dark faces, with their big eyes, as alike as brother and sister. Mitsou smiles, and the Blue Lieutenant smiles, and they look even more alike" (*M*, 654). Phil and Vinca share slender, unobtrusively muscular limbs and sunburned skins in *Ripening Seed* and the lovers in *Chance Acquaintances*, Lucette and Luigi, "belonged, as it were, to the same 'family group'. He really might have passed for her brother" (*CA*, 9).

The gender ambiguity of the desirable hero carries through to behaviour. He both acknowledges and endorses his status as object of desire by gestures conventionally coded feminine: Chéri preens in pearls, Jean coquettishly "prolongs his laugh in a canine grimace, with his lip curled up to show off his teeth" (*Cap*, 74), Michel displays a "totally physical seductiveness" developed thanks to years in professions where "he'd been forced to please both men and women" (*Duo*, 7). At the same time he has a privileged position to defend, and resents the woman's assumption of the role of subject: Herbert is outraged by Julie's dispassionate assessment of his step-son's charms "... I'm not going to have you discussing any male creature as if you were deciding to use it or not to use it!" (*JC*, 145) Alain is disconcerted by Camille's explicit desire for him "What ravages of desire on that face! Her mouth is quite distorted with it ... Who taught her to forestall me like that?" (*Cat*, 100), and Renée reflects that after they first make love Jean's eyes seem to "reproach (her) for something ... Perhaps he wanted me to be happy, but more respectful of his prowess, more broken, more vanquished" (*Cap*, 96).

The Colette heroine may suffer in her relationships with men, but she is unlikely to be broken or vanquished. The reversal of gender conventions that places male characters in the position of object also makes the subject female. Not only do women become subjects of the gaze, seeing men rather than being seen, but the female body itself is perceived to an important extent, subjectively, as a signifier of identity, as a set of appetites and desires, as the medium of relationship with the world – though this does not exclude a lucid recognition of the body's place as object of desire.

The central female protagonists are, on the whole, beautiful but the definition of beauty changes when the female body is no longer perceived as primarily sexual. The body shape of Colette's heroines varies: some are androgynously slender (Claudine, Mitsou, Vinca, Gigi), some are tall, slim but solidly built (Camille, Alice, Julie), some statuesque (Léa, Mme Haume, Mme Suzanne), and some plump and rounded (Fanny, the younger Sido). What the women share is a certain robustness: their bodies are strong and resistant to illness, and a variety of features connote adaptability and a healthy energy: eyes that subtly change colour with the surrounding light and according to mood, pink gums and good sets of teeth, solid necks, breasts that may sag slightly with age but which maintain their "half-apple" shape, strong legs and feet.

Features more traditionally valued in women as sexually desirable, that is, from an implictly male perspective come to be primarily valued as indicators of good health and of *joie-de-vivre*. Inevitably in Colette's textual world, where the boundaries of gender are never fixed, women's bodies may also rejoice in some qualities conventionally coded masculine: Julie's "strong deft hands" (*JC*, 80), "freedom from a single ounce of extra flesh" (*JC*, 96), "horsewoman's muscles" (*JC*, 143) and "long, clean-cut legs" (*JC*, 182) contrast with Herbert's signs of femininity, his "over-silky hair . . . curled like a woman's" (*JC*, 141) and his relative immobility, but the "masculine" signifiers also combine harmoniously with Julie's well-shaped breasts and delicate colouring so that gender signs are redistributed rather than merely exchanged.

Like male characters, female characters are essentially constructed by physical description in Colette's texts. Since, in many of the texts, women are positioned as subjects, either as first person narrators (*The Vagabond, The Captive*, many of the short stories) or as the main focaliser (*Chéri, The Other One*, and several more) a number of different narrative devices may be employed to allow an external focus on the body whilst maintaining the heroine as subject. In several cases Colette simply switches focalisation to another character or to an extradiegetic narrator so that, for example, Michel focalises the initial description of Alice, Jane that of Fanny, the narrator that of Gigi. In other cases the description is at least partially focalised through the heroine herself, as here:

> As for her body – "Everyone knows", Léa would say, "that a well-made body lasts, for a long time." She could still afford to show her body, pink and white, endowed with the long legs and straight back of a naiad on an Italian fountain; the dimpled hips, the high-slung breasts, "would last", Léa used to say, "till well after Chéri's wedding." (*C*, 19)

Here Léa's body is established in the text as both conforming to established criteria of female beauty (resembling a decorative statue) and as expressive of strength and resilience (long, straight, well-made), whilst the emphasis remains on Léa herself as subject. This effect is achieved elsewhere by the use of the mirror: Renée, Léa, Fanny, Julie all interrogate their own reflections and thus provide their own self-description in the text. Julie de Carneilhan, like all Colette's heroines untroubled by modesty, answers the telephone naked and thus comes to see, in the looking-glass, the reflection of:

> . . . a tall, naked woman . . . watching her . . . the colour of a yellow tea-rose, with the rather spare, flat belly of a barren woman, a pretty navel placed high at her middle and breasts that had lost none of their fineness, except in her own severely critical eyes. "Just a shade more like jelly-fish than apples cut in half these days" was her verdict. (*JC*, 122)

Here again the heroine contemplates her body both with pride – it confirms her sense of identity – and with the critical lucidity that acknowledges external criteria of feminine beauty.

Léa and Julie's frank assessment of their sexual assets is one aspect of the texts' uncensorious attention to physical reality. The ethereal heroines of the romantic imagination could not be further away: the appetite for life that is so marked a feature of these women starts, for example, with an appetite for good food. Like Alice in *Duo* they tend to eat "hungrily and quickly" (*T*, 88) even – or especially – in the midst of emotional crisis, and to consider food worthy of proper attention: "No arguments while we're eating. Paragraph Three of the Code Toutounier" (*T*, 155). Attendant problems of elimination, and of the quality of sanitary facilities, are not completely absent from the texts either, though any discussion of them provokes acute embarrassment in the male characters. The narrator of the music-hall texts devotes a brief and elegant article to the dark, malodorous closets provided for the *artistes* in provincial theatres with their "gaping pits more hideous than secret dungeons; an acrobat would think twice before trying to use one!";[4] both Alice and Léa offend their male partners by suggesting a connection between the state of their emotions and that of their intestines.

The body enters the text complete with parts and functions more commonly excluded from literary discourse. In the passage in *The Evening Star* which recalls the beauty of Colette's new-born daughter, the child's "assembled marvels" include not only nails and lashes but "the small sex, a barely incised almond, a bivalve precisely closed, lip to lip" (*ES*, 137). In the fiction, the heroines' sexuality is neither absent nor the central focus of characterisation: it is an integral part of female identity.

Sexual desire is experienced as a perfectly legitimate form of appetite, so that the seventeen-year-old Claudine is surprised to discover that illness reduces her interest in sex, and Minne spends the second half of *The Innocent Libertine* in search of an orgasm, fulminating against the lovers who fail to provide it: "He steals that pleasure from me! It's mine, mine . . . I want that ecstasy – or else that he should stop having it through me!" (*IL*, 118). Submissive little Annie leaves her conventional husband to spend her life in a quest for "fresh young bodies", and

Léa is quite frank about her initial reasons for carrying Chéri off to the country "But then, you know," she tells the embarrassed boxing coach she has employed to get Chéri into shape "I didn't take him on for his boxing" (*C*, 39).

The majority of Colette's heroines remain childless, by choice and because of their circumstances, but clearly the possibility of bearing children is another aspect of women's physical lives that determines how the body is represented. Illegitimate pregnancies and illegal abortions are part of the lives of the female music-hall artists, becoming central themes in "Gribiche" and "Bastienne's Child". Though Gribiche, despite the marked solidarity of her music-hall comrades, eventually dies of her abortion, the emphasis in "Bastienne" and in Colette's articles that deal with maternity is on the toughness and resilience of the female body, so that the "Colette" narrator of "Maternity" ("Maternité", 1945) spends her pregnancy engaged in her usual pursuits "which consisted of travelling by train or car, playing in pantomime and dancing"[5] and realises she is in labour whilst busy watering the garden. Bastienne dances on stage well into her pregnancy, with only a slight decrease in speed ("Why! I'm not ailing" [*CSC*, 148]), gives birth to a tiny Bastienne "hardy as a weed" (*CSC*, 149) and provides a vivid image of serene, active motherhood:

> Without waiting to sit down or unfasten her low-cut bodice, she uses both hands to free from its pressure a swollen breast, blue in colour from its generous veins. Leaning over, one foot lifted in the dancer's classical pose, her flared skirts like a luminous wheel around her, she suckles her daughter. (*CSC*, 149)

There is a potentially ironic contrast here between women's unromantic sense of their own corporeal selves, and the roles they are asked to play as sexualised bodies for display, a contrast made particularly acute by the fact that for most of Colette's heroines making a living is dependent upon the asset of their good looks and ability to provoke desire. These conflicting interpretations of the body are the source of some humour in the texts and of some sharp poignancy. It is in the music-hall texts that the contrast is most visible. The skinny, underfed little "Misfit" mounts the stage as an "elegant diner" in a Montmartre cabaret (*CSC*, 174), the series of gaudily decorated, semi-naked dancers at the nightclub in "La Fenice" reveal to the narrator's eye their "red wrists under a coat of wet white, on hands hardened by cooking, washing, and sweeping" (*CSC*, 183) and the acrobat is "undisguisedly pregnant" and "appears to find her act a torture" (182). The five little dancers of "The Workroom" ("L'Ouvroir", 1913) reveal their scars and wounds, their "non-existent breasts" (*CSC*, 118) and dirty underwear, as they remove the glamorous costumes in the shared dressing room. And it is not only on stage that the female body must be re-coded to conform to the conventions of male desire: Gigi's education consists of learning a complex set of rules about the presentation of the female body, and her healthy energy must be constrained by clothing that will draw attention to her body by concealing it: "she tried every dodge to free her lovely strong neck from its whale-bone collar of 'imitation Venetian point'" (*G*, 39).

The gap between body as experience and body as display is most acute in the story "Gribiche", where the music-hall dancer Gribiche, pregnant and unmarried, suffers an induced miscarriage backstage and leaves a trail of "little stars of fresh blood" (*CSC*, 212) amongst the sequins, the gaudy costumes and the bustle of the dressing rooms. At the end of the story another dancer Carmen, who has feared a similarly unwanted pregnancy, discovers that she is not pregnant after all, but must weep her tears of relief without damaging the mask that makes her into a stage woman:

> Armed with a little tube of blotting paper the size of a pencil, she was pressing it first to her right eyeball, then to her left, between the lids . . . "It's just that I'm awfully relieved. Fancy, I was six days late . . ." (*CSC*, 230)

Aging is another peril to be negotiated by the female body, but here the distinction between the body as subjective experience and the body as perceived by others again comes into play: the aging of the female body is seen as a process of degeneration in Colette's texts only where it is perceived through the lense of male desire. Léa's aging is painful, indeed tragic, for Chéri to whom her richly sexual and maternal body represented the only source of happiness. For Léa there is a difficult period of transition, but the body goes on, changed in its meanings but able to replace one set of pleasures with another, one rhythm of being with a different one. Thus too the narrator of *Break of Day* can look at her hand "which proclaims my age" and positively like its signs of experience "the skin . . . getting rather loose round the joints and on the back", its "scars and scratches" (*BD*, 37–8).

Renée only agonises over her age when she imagines Max, in the future, perceiving her as no longer beautiful, no longer the woman he loved: "Imagine me, still beautiful but desperate, frantic in my armour of corset and frock, under my make-up and powder . . ." (*V*, 170). Sido's vigorous energy negates the simple distinction between youth and age, so that her daughter reverses the difference between their ages: "In her company, I had to pretend to be almost as young as she was . . ." ("Rainy Moon", *CSC*, 372).

In the 1970s and 80s feminist writers have identified the

near absence in literature of a female perspective on the female body, and identified this absence as a crucial element in women's linguistic repression. Annie Leclerc in *Woman's Word* (1974) asserted the need to generate an alternative, female discourse by "talk(ing) about the pleasures of (the female) body",[6] which have been negated, devalued under a patriarchal culture: "only by talking about it will a new language be born, a woman's word." In a sense Colette's writing foreshadows Leclerc's theory, for her representation of the body goes serenely against the grain of literary convention. The body has always functioned as a signifier of identity but here the body becomes the primary mode of characterisation, inseparable from identity, determining the patterns of attraction and repulsion, of similarity and contrast that structure the narratives. As for gender, Colette's texts reverse, redistribute and assign new meanings to familiar physical signifiers of masculinity and femininity. The presence of a female subject as narrator or as the main focaliser produces a singularly sensual vision of the male body, and presents the specific features of the female body not as obstacles to be overcome in the project of being human, nor as assets solely dependent for their value on male appreciation, but as signs of strength and aspects of what Yannick Resch terms "women's . . . will to participate positively in the natural order of the universe" ("Corps feminin", 143).

6 Green Sealing Wax: Language, Style and Gender

The relationship between gender and language is a crucial question for feminist literary theory, and has been particularly central to the writing of French theorists. For Jacques Lacan, whose interpretations of and commentaries on the writings of Freud provide a starting point for the work of Hélène Cixous and Julia Kristeva, the child becomes a human subject precisely at the point of language acquisition, when s/he distinguishes between the self and what is not the self, and thus takes up a position within the Symbolic code (language). The recognition of the self as located within an external code, as "I", "you" or "s/he", is termed the "mirror stage", and coincides with the establishment of specifically human identity. The Symbolic code operates by distinguishing between one thing and another, by the principle of difference, and in this process the original term, or the primary signifier, is the phallus.

According to Lacan's theory the function of the phallus as primary signifier means that from the moment of becoming a subject the human being is gendered, because the relationship of the male and female child to the phallus is inevitably different. Though it is difficult to establish precisely what relationship Lacan assumes between the physical penis and the symbolic phallus, Lacanian theory certainly appears to establish a primary gender difference in that the very principle of language defines the masculine as the positive term, the feminine as the negative, as that which is not the phallus. On this theory, women's relationship to the Symbolic code must always and inherently be problematic, in that they speak from the position of the negative, of that which is silenced or repressed. It is clearly quite possible to move from this psychoanalytical theory to a theory of cultural exclusion, and we are not far from Dale Spender's "man-made language"[1] and the identification of a need to find linguistic modes of expression for the feminine and to challenge a linguistic formulation of the world that privileges the masculine. However, on Lacan's theory, this presents an insuperable theoretical problem, for there is no pre-discursive truth, no position from which to contest a linguistic code which does not merely signify a pre-existing reality but creates reality.

Kristeva presents a possible way forward in that she posits the existence of a space, or a time, which precedes the entry into the Symbolic but which may continue to have meaning for the subject. This pre-verbal stage, marked by identification with the mother's body, "previous and necessary to the acquisition of language but not identical to language", is termed the "semiotic", and its traces may appear in the text in the form of "a space, underlying the written . . . rhythmic, unfettered, irreducible to its intelligible, verbal translation".[2]

Whilst the "semiotic" would not be the exclusive realm of the woman writer, since all human subjects share the same fundamental drama of identification with and separation from the maternal body, it could be associated particularly with the feminine, both because it precedes the Symbolic's assignment of the feminine to the negative term, and because it brings the maternal body into the signifying process. If, as Terry Eagleton explains it, the "semiotic" is "a process *within* our conventional sign systems, which questions and transgresses their limits" and challenges "the phallus (as) symbol of sure, self-identical truth"[3] then the "semiotic" may be a useful category through which to consider the inscription of the feminine in women's writing.

The implication of Kristeva's theory here is that an articulation of the feminine may mean the disruption of both linguistic and literary forms, that the Symbolic code itself is, as Annie Leclerc termed it "man's word"[4] and that the semiotic may provide the formal possibility of articulating a "woman's word". Hélène Cixous writes of women writing "from 'without', from the heath where witches are kept alive; from below, from beyond 'culture'; from their childhood which men have been trying desperately to make them forget . . .".[5]

Both in language itself and in the codes of meaning that are produced by literary genres, a recurring feminist argument identifies the articulation of the feminine with disruption, subversion, a necessary flight from convention. If there is a danger here, it is that of a return to the gender essentialism which feminism began by contesting: women's writing would be identified with incoherence, disorder and uncontrolled emotionality to the exclusion of those qualities which bespeak control of the Symbolic code: formal precision, humour, varied modulation of tone and meaning.

The positive point of such theories, however, is that they provide a critical framework within which to examine specific relationships between sexual and textual politics (as Toril Moi's title nicely phrased it).[6] In Colette's case, this means examining language and gender in the texts in terms of both theme and form. Colette's writing itself thematises the relationship between language and gender, so that the nature of the Symbolic code, and the different places occupied by men and women in relation to language, may be explored as a recurring preoccupation in her work. But also, whilst it would be inappropriate to try to define such a skilled manipulator of language primarily in terms of the "semiotic", Colette's characteristic style does have distinct elements of the disruptive, for it disturbs comfortable relationships between signifier and signified and between the terms of those "scrupulous binary oppositions"[7] on which the Symbolic order is founded.

The theme of language takes the form of a recurring distinction between male and female discourse. Male characters in Colette's texts tend to assume a linguistic authority, a confident ability to name and categorise the world, that may operate at the level of speech or of the written word. Their confidence rests implicitly on the knowledge that their codes of meaning are those of the dominant discourse: the power to name means the power to define, to bring into existence or conversely, to silence and repress. Women are named by men, their social identity bestowed by husband or lover. The "Colette" of *Break of Day* refers to the author's own succession of linguistic identities before she achieved the freedom to name herself: first concealed completely in her texts behind the name "Willy", then Colette Willy, then Colette de Jouvenel, and at last "it came about that both legally and familiarly, as well as in my books, I now have only one name, which is my own. Did it take only thirty years of my life to reach that point, or rather to get back to it?" (*BD*, 19).

Marco in "The Képi" is called Marco because her name was Leonie before she married an artist: "Leonie wasn't the right sort of name for V's wife" (*CSC*, 507). Mitsou's only name is given by the man who keeps her, and represents an acronym of the two companies he manages ("Minoteries Italo-Tarbaises" and "Scieries Orléanaises Unifieés", flour-mills and sawmills). Thus Mitsou's name signifies that she is her lover's property, though the text itself not only narrates Mitsou's accession to language through the writing of letters to the "Blue Lieutenant", it also refuses the Namer his "proper name" by designating him only as "*L'Homme Bien*" or the "Well-to-do Man".

Gigi's education, in the story of the same name, is an exercise in repression: Gigi is taught that if she is to survive economically, she must not attempt to express herself outside those codes of language, dress and behaviour which, in the dominant discourse, signify "femininity". Gigi's inclination to articulate spontaneous feeling and to clearly describe the career for which she is being groomed must be curbed, for "Calling people and things by their name has never done anyone any good" (*G*, 22) insists her grandmother, functioning here as representative and teacher of the patriarchal code which has determined her own identity.[8]

Men's control of language is envied and coveted by female characters, but is also undermined and contested within the text as inadequate to a complex, plural reality. The story "Green Sealing Wax" ("La Cire verte", 1943) presents this ambivalent view of language in humorously figurative form. Narrated by the author's textual alter ego "Colette", set in the family home when she was fifteen-years-old, this story weaves together a narrative of murder and forgery with the themes of female adolescence and maternal protection, but foregrounds the process of writing itself.

The "green sealing wax" of the title is just one of the desirable objects displayed on the desk of the narrator's father, who collects there all the paraphernalia of the writing process, from pens with nibs of varied sizes to "a lacquer bowl filled with a golden powder to dry the wet page" (*CSC*, 388), to early gadgets for making multiple copies. His daughter covets this wealth of tantalising objects and braves her father's possessive wrath to steal objects to add to her own collection or, in the case of sealing wafers, to eat, but whilst she thus attempts to share her father's figurative access to the written word, she also recognises the void that this conceals. Equipped with all the ceremonial signs of writing, the father rarely puts pen to paper, whereas Sido dispenses with all formal signs of linguistic production but produces texts whose close association with everyday reality is signified by the circumstances of their writing:

> sitting at any old table, pushing aside an invading cat, a basket of plums, a pile of linen, or else just putting a dictionary on her lap by way of a desk – Sido really did write. A hundred enchanting letters prove that she did. (*CSC*, 389)

Paternal access to language here is both enviable as a rich, varied resource, equipped with all that is necessary for the production of texts, and seen as ultimately empty, possessing less substance than the private, scribbled but communicative discourse of the mother. Perhaps it is significant too that Madame Hervouet, the story's murderess, tries to authenticate her forgery of her husband's will – a very bad forgery, in her woman's writing, wildly improbable in legal terms – by sealing it with the green sealing wax taken from Captain Colette's desk. The text comments ironically on the understandable but ultimately self-defeating temptation to simply appropriate male discourse.

The contrast between an authoritative, categorising male language and a more plural, tentative female voice recurs in several novels and stories. Max, in *The Vagabond* with his "prescriptive sense of normality"[9] is a black and white figure not only in terms of his physical characterisation, but also in his straightforwardly dualist vision of the world. When Renée packs her underclothes next to those of her male partner to save luggage space on tour it is "contemptible . . . sordid . . . promiscuous" (*V*, 142–3) and two women embracing are a "depraved couple" (161). Marriage, on the other hand, represents an appropriate destiny for a woman that can replace mere stop-gap careers "But, darling, you no longer need the music-hall now that I am there . . ." (*V*, 122). Renée's problem in coming to terms with Max is posed in specifically linguistic terms: "I don't know how to talk to you, poor Dufferein-Chautel. I hesitate between my own personal language . . . and the slovenly, lively idiom . . . which one learns in the music-hall . . . Unable to decide, I choose silence" (*V*, 70).

Farou of *The Other One* proposes his definitions of femininity and relationships not only in private but publicly on the stage, as a popular playwright, and his wife winces at the inaccurate simplicity of his version of a dialogue between two women.

> This time, Fanny listened, irreverently. "Perhaps he really thinks that's how it would be. He makes me laugh". (*OO*, 144)

Michel of *Duo* shocks Alice with the platitudinous certainties through which he attempts to understand her infidelity: "The funniest thing of all is that he believes it; he thinks he knows what a woman's desire is like" (*Duo*, 53). In "The Képi" the "Colette" narrator opposes her own sympathetic and complex characterisation of Marco to the crudely reductionist wit of Masson and Willy who greet her late discovery of the pleasures of love with cold cynicism: "Probably, like many women, our worthy Marco imagines she is the bride of Satan. It's the phase of infernal joys" comments Masson.

> I thought it detestable that either of her two friends should call Madame V. "our worthy Marco". Nor was I any more favourably impressed by the icily critical comments of these two disillusioned men, especially on anything concerning friendship, esteem or love." (*CSC*, 520)

These female responses to male discourse tend to be quietly ironic, to question the self-importance implicit in the male speaker/writer's representation of masculinity, and to question the accuracy of his characterisation of the feminine. The technique of the unspoken critique, scarcely articulated but sufficiently indicated to throw a perspective of female irony over the text, is carried to its logical conclusion in the "dialogues for one voice", texts in which the presence of "Colette" as silent participant in the conversation is indicated only by a row of dots or by the speaker's appeals to her. Thus in "An Interview" "Colette's" hostile reaction to the pompous journalist who interviews her without ever allowing her to speak, and reads his own assumptions into her enforced silence, is signified by his responses:

> What do you mean, you haven't opened your mouth? Except that in that expression there are a hundred lines of psychology. Isn't a woman entirely in what she doesn't say? (*CSC*, 44)

The same technique serves to challenge the masculine complacency of Chaveriat in "The Tender Shoot". Once the narration of his story is begun, the "Colette" who has elicted it by direct invitation and by loosening the speaker's tongue with best brandy, remains silent – but her critical response to Chaveriat's tactics as a seducer and to his way of defining his own behaviour is indicated in the text by Chaveriat's "Excuse me, what were you saying, my dear? That it was a horrid proceeding and a classical one?" (*CSC*, 427), and his "Begging your pardon, I am not a brute" (*CSC*, 436).

Men speak and write with the authority of the dominant culture: the least articulate of Colette's male characters are those, like Chéri, who have failed to properly assimilate the codes of masculine behaviour. Women's language, it is suggested, is less public, less rhetorical, more exploratory. There is, of course, a very fundamental contradiction here in that by their very presence the books demonstrate the existence of female-authored texts within the public world of discourse: the daughter "Colette" may have taken her mother's writing as "model" as she emphasises in *Break of Day* ("She gave me life and the mission to pursue those things which she, a poet, seized and cast aside as one snatches a fragment of a floating melody drifting through space" [*BD*, 25]), but she has also appropriated her father's writing equipment by bringing her texts into the public realm.

This dual relationship to language is acknowledged within the fiction, where despite the critical perspective on a public language largely identified as masculine, the imperative to write, and thus to assume the role of subject within the Symbolic code, is frequently a female concern. If Renée "the vagabond" rejects the very real temptation to seek fulfilment in Max's love, it is partly because love here is incompatible with writing "as if the one dominating anxiety in my life were to seek for words, words to express how yellow the sun is, how blue the sea, and how brilliant the salt like a fringe of white jet" (*V*, 176).

The "Colette" narrators of the stories "Bella Vista" and "Rainy Moon", like the narrator of *Break of Day*, are writers by profession as well as by their position in the text, motivated by what Renée defines as "a need, sharp as thirst in summer, to note and to describe" and engage in "the perilous and elusive task of seizing and pinning down . . . the many-hued, fugitive, thrilling adjective" (*V*, 13).

Even Colette's detractors have tended to acknowledge the quality of her style: she was, wrote the celebrated critic Gustave Lanson "one of the great stylists of the age".[10] What this means from the reader's point of view is that the pleasure of reading Colette lies less in the thrill of suspense and satisfaction provided by narrative, than in the contemplative, almost sensual delight of language itself. Colette's practice as a writer corresponds to her thematic treatment of language. She is both a skilful manipulator of the Symbolic code within its own terms, using language to name, represent, evoke a world as thrillingly varied as the articles on her father's desk, and she employs stylistic devices which correspond to Kristeva's "semiotic" in that they produce language "irreducible" to an intelligible signified, which accentuate the sensual pleasure of speech that precedes acquisition of the Symbolic for the infant. As the quotation from *The Vagabond* above suggests, Colette's writing is founded both on the principle of representation, the desire to "note and describe" and thus to achieve linguistic form for experience, and on the intratextual pleasures of playing with language as a system of sound and meaning.

There is a consistent element of what we might term successful realism in Colette's style, in the sense that her descriptions of place, character and objects produce in the reader that shock of recognition that greets the precise articulation of a known, or of an acutely plausible, reality. Though, in the fiction at least, description always has a thematic and/or narrative function, rather than simply providing a backdrop or reinforcing a sense of the real, it does create the illusion of the text as "mere transcription of reality".[11] When in *Ripening Seed*:

> An off-shore breeze wafted the scent of the new-mown after-crop, farmyard smells, and the fragrance of bruised mint; little by little, along the level of the sea, a dusty pink was usurping the domain of blue unchallenged since the early morning. (*RS*, 21)

the heady odours of the breeze and the gradual replacement of the colour blue by pink connote Phil's state of vulnerable sensuality, and herald the theme of alternative forms of love, but the precise sensory images also verbally represent a Breton seascape. In both *The Vagabond* and the much later "Rainy Moon", an urban street scene represents, for the narrator, the splendid variety of life outside the confines of obsessive love. In the earlier novel Renée is on tour in Marseilles and watches the happy, idle passers-by on a quay side street:

> there are fresh flowers, carnations tied up in stiff bunches, like leeks, soaking in green pails: there is a street-stall loaded with black bananas smelling of ether, violets, clams, blue mussels and cockles, dotted about with lemons and little flasks of pink vinegar. (*V*, 162–3)

whilst the narrator of "Rainy Moon" observes a busy shopping street that slopes up to Montmartre in Paris, and sees amongst the hung chickens and the false hair pieces:

> oranges piled up in formation like cannon-balls for ancient artillery, withered apples, unripe bananas, anemic chicory, glutinous wads of dates, daffodils, pink panties, bloomers encrusted with imitation Chantilly . . .

as well as "shapeless housewives . . . blondes in down-at-heel shoes and brunettes in curlers . . . mother-of-pearl smelts", "butcher boys with cherubic faces" (*CSC*, 361). Structured as lists that accumulate disparate objects, jumbling together colours, shapes, tastes and smells, both descriptions elide the banal with the beautiful, the inanimate with the human, in a celebration of what is termed elsewhere "the marvellous commonplace" (*CSC*, 366). At one level these passages function through classically realist techniques of accumulated detail and appeal to the senses, though their absence of any aesthetic hierarchy that would separate flowers from bloomers, and the emphasis on plurality and variety rather than unity, are typical of Colette.

It is already apparent in these passages that the device of analogy is central to Colette's descriptive style: the carnations are "tied up in stiff bunches like leeks", the bananas smell of ether, the oranges are piled like cannonballs and the butcher-boys' faces are like those of cherubs. Figures of speech based on analogy are features of standard linguistic practice, and offer a rich set of signifying possibilities. Colette employs simile and metaphor as devices which enhance descriptive precision – the visual image of the oranges is less exact without the analogy of cannonballs – and which signify beyond the descriptive: the carnations "like leeks", the "mother-of-pearl" fish, contribute to an overall refusal to distinguish between objects of beauty and objects for use.

This extensive use of analogy is equally important in the construction of characters, where again the function of the simile or metaphor tends to be both visually descriptive and indicative of thematic concerns. Analogy can condense meaning, providing in an economical way both a vivid indication of physical appearance and a signifier of the character's function in the text's system of meaning: it is thus of particular value in the short story, where character must be rapidly established, and in the case of minor characters who again, need to be constructed for the reader with a relative economy of means. Thus Madame Hervouet of "Green Sealing Wax" owes her clear visual characterisation to her "resemblance to a black-and-yellow wasp" (*CSC*, 392), an image which also establishes the repressed anger and passion that will lead to her final undoing.

In the story "Toutouque" in *My Mother's House* the central character is a dog, but a dog whose transformation from equable, affectionate family pet to wild fury under the influence of sexual passion, clearly has a human significance. The sensitive and wholly charming character of Toutouque is established through a rapid series of similes and metaphors: she is "broad and squat as a four-months pigling", but has delicate "shell-like" ears, with warm eyes "the color of old Madeira" like those of "a mulatto woman", and she displays a "nanny-like" amiability. Thus the shock of seeing Toutouque as a "kind of bristling yellow monster" (*MMH*, 98) is prepared.

Odette of "The Rendez-vous" with her strong white teeth and cruel wit is a "cannibal"; the grotesque old woman in "The Burglar" ("Le Cambrioleur", 1924) who still dresses and acts like a beautiful young girl has a face like "a death's head in make-up", "pink as a piece of cracked wax fruit" (*CSC*, 271), images which establish the hideous visual contrast between decay and artifice. The same strongly visualised contrast occurs in the minor character of old Lili in *Chéri*: the embodiment of Léa's worst fears about aging, but also a member of the cast of characters representing the *demi-monde* of 1900, Lili's disturbing concealment of an aging body beneath signifiers of youthful sexuality is expressed partly through analogies: she has "the corpulence of a eunuch", "a skinny bosom crinkled like the wattles of a turkey-cock" a neck "the shape of a flower-pot and the size of a belly" (*C*, 56).

In the case of the novels and of the major characters, the system of analogy tends to extend beyond the level of the individual simile or metaphor, and to become an integral part of the texts' system of meaning, taking us to another level of analysis. Chéri, for example, is associated throughout the novel with a cluster of non-human images: demon, god, blackbird, Asiatic prince, savage which establish the form and the impact of his beauty whilst signifying his alienation from the dominant culture, just as the consistent comparison of Farou (*The Other One*) to a wild animal establishes both his sexual magnetism and his human inadequacy.

Several novels set up internal metaphors, where a system of mutual comparison refers character to setting, and setting back to character. Léa is partially constructed as a character through the image of her welcoming, well-tended household with its dominant shade of pink but the house, in turn, and the colour pink, come to signify Léa even in her absence. The great indestructible leather sofa "le toutounier" is the place where Alice and her sisters talk, sleep, offer mutual love and support, but it then comes to mean all of these things, and the promise of their renewal, when Alice is left alone. Vinca with her "periwinkle eyes" and blonde hair "like stiff corn-stalks glinting in the sun" (*RS*, 5) is both a strongly visualised character and, through her identification with the natural world, part of a complex network of figurative meanings that unify the novel. Colette's use of the "indirect discourse"[12] of the image, and particularly of colour imagery, has been thoroughly analysed elsewhere and does not need lengthy discussion here.[13]

The purpose above has been to identify the referential qualities of Colette's style, those qualities which produce a convincing evocation of a world both tangible and suffused with meanings, through the use of familiar linguistic techniques of accumulated sensory detail and of analogy. This imples some optimism about existing forms of language as a resource for the woman writer: that rigidity and reductionism that Colette associates thematically with male discourse would seem not to be a feature of language itself, but merely a particular, and avoidable, style of language. "The round material world, crammed with savours" (*BD*, 111) may be experienced and communicated within the medium of the Symbolic code. There are, nonetheless, two crucial features of Colette's style which invite discussion in terms of Kristeva's category of the "semiotic", and both of them lead towards the figure of the mother, of "Sido", that lies at the heart of Colette's work.

Though Colette's analogies are very frequently unexpected, like the Swiss lake in *The Captive* "the colour of a sick pearl" (*Cap*, 59) or the cat's "yawn like a flower" (*BD*, 15) in *Break of Day*, the rational basis for the analogy can generally be deduced. Occasionally the frontier of logic is passed and an image produces, instead of a sudden perception of resemblance, that spark of incongruity sought by the Surrealists,[14] as when Fanny is described by Farou as "white as a coloured girl" (*OO*, 38), or the shadow of white trees is as "blue as young corn".[15]

Colette's writing favours the paradoxical, the disturbance, through apparently contradictory associations of words, of meanings which our culture holds to be rational and self-evident. Stupidity, in Colette's texts, may be "sublime" (*CSC*, 206), Chéri's lack of intelligence or education gives him "majesty" (*LC*, 211), he is "magnificent and inferior" (*LC*, 211). The parents in *Ripening Seed* have the "childishness" and "faith in a rosy future" (*RS*, 40) which Phil and Vinca in their adolescent wisdom, envy, and Camille is never so pitiable a character as when she has just tried to murder Saha in *The Cat*, "poor little murderess" (*Cat*, 132). "Impetuosity" in "The Képi" has its own peculiar rituals (*CSC*, 527) and the "The Hidden Woman" ends her story in a glorious state of "immodest innocence" (*CSC*, 238).

The most frequent forms of linguistic paradox are those which involve the transposition of gender signs. From Phil's "traits . . . of a violated girl" (*RS*, 61), Vinca's "virile contempt" (*RS*, 66) and Camille's "soft, masculine voice" (*RS*, 45) in *Ripening Seed*, a novel that operates a constant exchange of gender signs between the three central characters, to Julie de Carneilhan's "shocking and masculine gesture(s)" (*JC*, 182) and her lover Coco's resemblance to "one of those old fashioned French girls" (*JC*, 116), Colette's writing is characterised by a deliberate and playful displacement of the signifiers of masculinity and femininity.

The questioning of accepted meanings through paradox and contradiction is particularly associated with Sido. The style of speech and writing that Colette attributes to her "model" Sido in *Break of Day* is paradoxical because it denies the most fundamental dualities in the name of a celebratory sense of wholeness and unity. Faithful, monogamous heterosexual love is one of the major positive values of our culture but "So great a love!" writes Sido of her husband's life-long devotion to her, "What frivolity!" (*BD*, 127), and in another letter evoked in the same text "Love is not a sentiment worthy of respect" (*BD*, 22). For love, as her daughter comments, "suppresses and condemns everything around it" (*BD*, 133). Sido also "knew that one possesses through abstaining, and only through abstaining" (*BD*, 24) and refused the distinction between good and evil for "evil and good can be equally resplendent and fruitful" (*BD*, 27). Youth and age cease to be opposites: "Seventy-five? . . . it's not true is it? Must one really soon give up being young?" writes Sido.

> No, no, of course not, don't give it up yet – I've never known you anything but young, your death saves you from growing old and even from dying, you who are always with me. (*BD*, 91)

The structure of *Break of Day* echoes the paradox, for Sido who was Colette's point of origin becomes in turn her destination, and the distinction between birth and death is itself questioned by the placing of the mother at the end as well as at the beginning. This refusal of the most fundamental dualities of language, particularly in its correspondence with a powerful image of the mother as source of a re-found unity, seems to belong with the "semiotic" as that force which "questions and transgresses ... the limits of our conventional sign systems". In the words of Nicole Ward-Jouve "Difference is no longer the absolute corner-stone."[16]

There is another sense too in which the "semiotic" is relevant to Colette's writing. The Symbolic code works through an assumption of clear and fixed relationships between verbal signifier and the signified: though the relationship between sound and sense is in fact, on the whole arbitrary, a functional use of language requires that we suppress awareness of that arbitrary coding and proceed as if "dog" meant, in some immutable way, "dog". The semiotic, in as far as it originates in that pre-verbal period when sounds were pleasurable without fixed meanings, could be said to free the signifier from the signified, as in certain forms of poetry.

There is a distinct preoccupation in Colette's texts with the word as sensual experience, with the materiality of language or what the writer herself calls "phonetic rapture" (*JM*, 83). The child astride the garden wall plays with the multiple possibilities of the word "presbytery" "with its harsh and spiky beginning and the brisk trot of its final syllables" (*MMH*, 45), shouting it at invisible outlaws "Begone! you are all presbyteries!", and then deciding that it "might very possibly be the scientific term for a certain little yellow-and-black striped snail". To learn that the word is limited to the sole signified of "a priest's house" can only be a disappointment. It is a child too who, in the story "The Sick Child" ("L'Enfant malade", 1944) frees words from their functional limits to experience them as sound, smell, or image, so that his robust cousin Charlie's use of the word "boy-scout" is "half-steel, half India-rubber" (*CSC*, 336), and when he hears his mother and the doctor discussing his possibly salutary "crisis":

> Sometimes it entered ceremoniously, like a lady dressed up to give away prizes with an h behind its ear and a y tucked into its bodice: Chrysis, Chrysis Wilby-Sallatry . . . (*CSC*, 339)

The sick child rides on words, meets them as monsters "pointed sounds with muzzles like mongooses" (*CSC*, 341), hears their music, and since good health will restore him to a structured life and a functional perception of language, the story's "happy ending" is only qualified and he falls asleep "assenting, cured and disappointed" (*CSC*, 346). The adult narrator of *Break of Day* retains some sense of the sensual variety of words:

> Solitary . . . it's a beautiful-looking word, beginning with its capital S rearing like a protective serpent. I can't entirely isolate it from the fierce glitter it receives from the solitaire diamond . . . (*BD*, 67)

and the narrator of *Journey for Myself: Selfish Memories* (*Le Voyage egoiste*, 1922) feverishly hot, delights not just in the thought but in the word "frost" (*givre* in French): "When I repeat that sparkling word, I feel that I'm biting into a crunchy ball of snow" (*JM*, 20). Chéri's incantatory use of the name "Nounoune" for Léa is surely also based on the sensual pleasure of the repeated syllable, and resembles the first sounds that babies make, intensifying the sense that for Chéri loving Léa means a return to the semiotic.

The "semiotic" means the carrying forward, into adult life and adult discourse, of a lost unity preceding identity, preceding difference. If the Symbolic code is identified with the masculine, because of the status of the phallus as positive term, then the semiotic can well be seen as the potentially disruptive power of the suppressed feminine. The problem is that this locates the feminine in a backward-looking search for total fusion with the mother, when the achievement of adult identity requires both identification and differentiation. To see the semiotic as the only authentic source of a "woman's word" seems to exclude women from the realm of written language, except where writing is at the very frontiers of intelligible meaning.

Colette's writing demonstrates a woman's highly competent, and confident, assumption of the role of subject within the Symbolic code, whilst thematically addressing the issue of male control of language, and whilst introducing a dimension that could usefully be related to the "semiotic". Particularly through the figure of Sido, but also through consistent aspects of her style, Colette disturbs the comfortable polarities of language and the unquestioned relationship of signifier to signified. Sido does not represent only the nostalgic reality of a pre-symbolic past, but also represents a movement forwards, which integrates and transcends the rational world identified with the father. It is Sido who first takes the green sealing wax from her husband's desk and offers it to her daughter; it is Sido who, in her daughter's recreation, writes letters which are both intelligible and suffused with an interrogation of standard meanings, and it is she who in her final letter before her death leaves the constrictions of language behind not to regress, but to advance. The two sheets she addressed to her daughter (in *Break of Day*) contain few words, only "joyful signs" and embryonic sketches which echo the book's dominant metaphor of blossoming, shining outwards: "arrows emerging from an embryo word, little rays" (*BD*, 142). These represent:

> messages from a hand that was trying to transmit to me a new alphabet or the sketch of some ground-plan envisaged at dawn under rays that would never attain the sad zenith.

and if her daughter can pursue the signs then she will gain access to the disparate, wonderfully various plurality of meaning signified by the book's closing images: "a quickset hedge, spindrift, meteors, an open and unending book, a cluster of grapes, a ship, an oasis . . ." (*BD*, 143).

7 Break of Day and The Evening Star

Colette's fictions take place in a patriarchal world where power is gendered masculine. Once her heroines step outside the structures of female dependence, they have practical problems of economic survival. They may also have emotional and sexual problems, for whilst they form heterosexual relationships out of love or desire for an individual, the institution of marriage, or even that of the love affair, has its own rules and assumptions which equate female love with submission.

The representations of femininity which have currency are authored by men: the women who work in the music-hall know very well how artificial are the glamorised, sanitised bodies that signify "Woman" on the stage, but they need their pay at the end of the week. Fanny and Jane recognise the utter inaccuracy of Farou's version of female dialogue, but he is the celebrated playwright on whom, moreover, they both depend. Given the cultural dominance of male visions of femininity, many Colette heroines also have problems of identity, for how are they to assume their own strength and independence when the only available images of these qualities are masculine? The "Colette" of *The Pure and the Impure* (*Le Pur et l'impur*, 1932) recalls how she worried about "the masculine streak in my character" and tried hard to rid herself of "this ambiguity" in order to offer to the man she wanted "a healthy and quite female body and its perhaps fallacious vocation of servant" (*PI*, 56).

However, a reading of almost any of her works demonstrates that despite their exclusion from power, despite their vulnerability in a male-authored culture, women are the survivors in Colette's world.

> . . . a woman can never die of grief. She is such a solid, creature, so hard to kill! (*V*, 27)

> Once again I find myself exclaiming: "What a solid creature a woman is!"[1]

With few exceptions (Renée in *The Captive*, Marco in "The Kepi", Gigi) it is the women who emerge from the novels with their appetite for life intact, the men who retreat into the past or even die. Men and women in Colette's work, have fundamentally different ways of relating to the world and others, and this difference produces a curious contradiction whereby the sex who are disadvantaged socially and politically are better equipped for emotional survival, and even for happiness, than their dominant brothers. Colette's fictional world looks forward here to the scenarios of emotional development suggested by feminist re-interpretations of Freud, and can usefully be read, for example, in the light of Nancy Chodorow's theory of gender in *The Reproduction of Mothering* (1978).

Chodorow argues that in a society where parenting is almost exclusively a maternal role, both male and female children begin life with a profound attachment to and identification with the mother, but that the acquisition of masculine and feminine identity inevitably produces different emotional structures. The boy, in order to identify with the father and achieve the goal of masculinity, must thoroughly repress his pre-Oedipal relation with the mother and emphasise his separation and distinctness. This leaves him wary of emotional relationships, of anything that may recall his early identification with the mother and hence with the feminine, but exclusively directed towards women as erotic objects. Girls, on the other hand, must continue to identify with the mother who is also their gender model, and thus negotiate a complex process of simultaneous connection and differentiation. Their experience of self remains that of self in relationship, their sense of connectedness to other women survives the transition to genital heterosexuality and means that whilst:

> most women emerge from their Oedipus complex erotically heterosexual – that is, oriented to the father and men as primary erotic objects – heterosexual love and emotional commitment are less exclusively established. Men tend to remain emotionally secondary. (*Chodorow*, 167)

This corresponds quite closely to Colette's representation of men and women, for in her world men tend to have a self-conscious, somewhat theatrical sense of their own masculinity, a desire to reduce the complexity of relationship to a simple system of exchange, and – in some cases – a tenuous and fragile hold on life. It is as if they have failed to internalise the mother's love, whereas the women protagonists are securely connected to the world via a network of female attachments and a continuing relation with a mother-figure who may be literally their mother, or her metaphorical representation, or simply an internalised sense of the maternal.

Colette's female characters are critical of the element of display in masculinity, of men's tendency to play to the gallery. In order to see themselves and to be seen as successfully masculine, her heroes must act out their autonomy, repress weakness, assume the power and authority their culture attributes to the male. Like the tomcats of Colette's animal texts, "more noisy than really warlike",[2] from a female perspective male protagonists can appear posturing, more concerned with the image they present than the emotional reality of the relationship. When Farou finds himself confronted with Fanny's knowledge of his affair with Jane, his immediate response is theatrical ("All the better", said Farou with great dignity. "My place is here. Let's get all this settled" [*OO*, 145]) then turns immediately to concern for public opinion.

> I can be sure that nothing which concerns the three of us will give rise to public scandal? Not even to servants' gossip? (*OO*, 145)

Fanny finds his ceremonious manner at dinner comical.

> I don't know why, but tonight you look like a young tragic actor playing a comedy part! (*OO*, 148)

Michel, faced with Alice's infidelity, reacts with the same combination of role-playing and anxiety about appearances. His real pain at betrayal is externalised as "the dignity of an offended husband . . . tinged with meekness and caution" which leads Alice to mutter irritably "He's an actor, a third-rate actor like all men" (*Duo*, 34), and she finds his "play-acting for the sake of a servant . . . beneath contempt" (*Duo*, 26). The narrator of *Ripening Seed* describes Phil with a mixture of sympathy and gently deflating irony when he dramatises his predicament as a young man trapped by the constraints of childhood.

> He radiated intolerance and a sort of traditional despair. In his haste to grow up . . . this scion of a small Parisian industrial house was transformed into a hero of romance. (*RS*, 18)

Male characters often attempt to manage relationships by operating a simple emotional economy, based on the system of exchange that prevails in the public, male-ordered world. They believe, that is, that if they pay the right price they will receive the love or the gratification they desire. Damien, one of the Don Juan figures of *The Pure and the Impure*, comes to resemble for the narrator "another haggling trader, disappointed in a bargain" (*PI*, 49) as he laments the discrepancy between the amount of sexual pleasure he has given and received.

Chaveriat of "The Tender Shoot" attempts to seduce Louisette by offering her gifts, a strategy the narrator classifies as "a horrid proceeding, and a classic one" (*CSC*, 427), and one which Louisette herself utterly refuses. It is also Gaston's strategy in *Gigi* and one attempted by Coco in *Julie de Carneilhan*. Michel of *Duo* believes that Alice has failed in her side of the bargain by being unfaithful, and therefore "deserves" to be unhappy. His dialogue with Alice exemplifies the gap between male and female moralities in the field of relationships:

> "Why should you be happy when you don't deserve to be?"
>
> "Because I want to be."
>
> "That's a fine reason!"
>
> "It's the best one. You're talking to me about what I deserve! What has deserving got to do with the need to take deep breaths, have a good complexion and not punish yourself every morning." (*Duo*, 104)

If, in the Freudian scenario, the fear of castration is the stick that drives the male child to resolve the Oedipal conflict, the carrot that draws him on is the power and authority associated with being like Daddy. But within a relationship masculinity as authority depends on femininity as submission and respect. A recurring scene in Colette's fiction shows the discomfiture of the male hero when faced with female irreverence: Jean suffers from Renée's failure to be "more broken, more vanquished" (*Cap*, 96) when they first make love, and later from "the furious regret of not having created (her)" (*Cap*, 133). Phil waits to see Vinca appear at her window the morning after they first make love: "They're always said to weep, after" (*RS*, 119). But Vinca is singing, not weeping, and watering the fuchsia in a contented, everyday way. Phil is wounded by what he feels to be the negation of his own role:

> Neither a hero, nor yet an executioner . . . A little pain, a little pleasure . . . That's all I shall have given her, that and nothing else . . . nothing . . . (*RS*, 122)

And Alain is appalled by the cheerful nudity of his new wife, whose lack of shame seems to deny the importance of his male gaze:

> But what a . . . what brazenness. Does she think I'm dead? Or does it seem perfectly natural to walk about stark naked? (*Cat*, 83–4)

The most fragile of Colette's heroes radically enact the loss of identity, by suicide in the case of Michel (*Duo*) and Chéri, and by a withdrawal into the world of childhood in the case of Alain (*The Cat*). The stories of Chéri and Alain are in a sense stories of Oedipal failure, for in each narrative there is a clear representation of the mother: Léa, Chéri's beautiful, nurturing mistress, and in *The Cat* Alain's home garden with its constant fertility and "protective atmosphere" (152), and in each the hero attempts and fails to leave the maternal world and achieve adult masculinity through physical separation and through marriage. But Chéri and Alain are the casualties of patriarchy, unable to find happiness in an adult world which, seen from their perspective, looks cold and harsh and empty;

left with a desperate need for the maternal love they have been forced to abandon but have never internalised.

In *The Last of Chéri* the hero flees Edmée's "plethora of whiteness" (*LC*, 162) and her brisk, emancipated efficiency to seek the "incandescent rose-pink" (*LC*, 195) and the warmth he associates with the memory of Léa. But the passing years have transformed his mistress into a plump old woman with a life that excludes him, and Chéri takes refuge in the past before finally shooting himself amongst photos and relics of his lost and only love.

Alain's desire for Camille is mingled with resentful hostility from the outset, but it is her attack on the symbols of his childhood self, her appropriation of his room for their future child and her attempt to kill Saha, the cat, which at last drive him to return to the garden and renounce adulthood. In both novels the narratives' system of dual focalisation is crucial, for the reader both identifies with Alain and Chéri, seeing the adult world from their point of view as emotionally alien, and sees that from the perspective of Camille or Edmée, these heroes look inadequate and pathetically frail. Camille is only granted the position of focaliser at the very end of the novel, but the switch to her viewpoint as she leaves the garden reveals Alain in an infantile, scarcely human pose, dressed in outgrown pyjamas and lying "with one hand hollowed into a paw, . . . playing deftly with the first green prickly August chestnuts" (*Cat*, 157).

Michel too, bereft of his secure role as husband because Alice has casually committed what, in his terms, is an act of grave infidelity, finally walks to the edge of his property and into the river, "slow-moving and heavy with iron-red mud" (*Duo*, 131). This refusal to face the difficulty of the changed relationship, this flight into water, may also perhaps be seen as a renunciation of the Oedipal struggle and a return to the maternal.

Focalised by male protagonists anxious about their own

place in the world, Colette's women can appear robust and resilient to the point of brutality. Chéri faints from remembered desire for Léa: Edmée, dispenser of "carefully measured doses of love" (*LC*, 142), looks after him "efficiently, professionally" (*LC*, 173) and with one eye on the clock so as not to miss her next appointment. But when Chéri revisits Léa several years after their parting, only Léa's laughter and her blue eyes remain to show that this "healthy old woman . . . well able to carry her burden of flesh and freed from restraining stays" (*LC*, 184) is the Léa of his memory, and her conversation revolves placidly around his health, whether he is taking proper care of his kidneys, the importance of eating well.

> Romanticism, nerves, distaste for life: stomach. The whole lot, simply stomach. Love itself! (*LC*, 192)

From this point in the novel, Chéri's descent towards suicide is inevitable.

The same discrepancy between male emotional anguish and cheerful female pragmatism appears in *The Cat*, when Camille describes her plans for redecorating Alain's room as a nursery:

> Camille was calmly proceeding with her woman's life among the wreckage of Alain's past. (*Cat*, 120)

and Michel wonders that Alice can sleep and eat so well in the midst of their crisis, when he has lost all appetite. Colette does not replace the powerful dualism of patriarchal lore with a reversed dichotomy of positive women and negative men: narrative perspective quite frequently situates the reader with a hero whose emotional needs, although regressive and impossible, are sympathetically portrayed.

The narrative voice which dominates and unifies Colette's world is, nonetheless, female and in the context of patriarchal values, oppositional. Female protagonists are shocked by certain aspects of male behaviour in relationships: their tendency to reproduce the ethic of the market-place by demanding a precise reciprocity in love conflicts with the women's more complex and diffuse version of give and take. Léa laughs at Chéri's attempt to negotiate the finances of their first stay together in Normandy, and over the years of their relationship she simply gives, abundantly and without counting costs, surprised by the recognition that Chéri's role, in the parlance of their society, is that of a gigolo. The same philosophy makes her unable to comprehend why her friend Patron can not simply agree to be kept by his mistress, since she is the richer.

"Colette" is shocked by Chaveriat's attempt to pay for sexual favours with presents in "The Tender Shoot", and the story *Gigi* narrates the preparation of a young girl for an exchange system that rewards "femininity" with a luxurious lifestyle. If Gigi can learn all the appropriate codes of dress and behaviour including "a pretty little collection of weaknesses and a terror of spiders" described by Aunt Alicia as "our indispensable stock-in-trade with men" (*G*, 37) then Gaston will pay for her company with jewels, travel and an insurance policy. Gigi's largely unsuccessful project in the story is to place their relationship on a wholly different footing.

What distinguishes Colette's female characters, and particularly the most positive of them, is their relation to the maternal world. The maternal, in Colette's work, signifies the unqualified, undemanding love on which self-love, and a secure inner sense of identity, are founded. Whereas for many of the male characters the maternal, whether it be represented by a woman or by a symbolic place, is subject to loss and incompatible with adult masculinity, for the female protagonists the maternal world may be integrated into adult identity. Chapter two showed that the mythology of the Third Republic represented the maternal world as regressive, as needing to be sacrificed to maturity, and the dramas of Colette's male characters reproduce this pattern. But in the case of women, whilst the maternal may change form and be signified in a variety of ways, it continues to be an important element of female selfhood.

There is, of course, quite literally a central figure of the mother in Colette's texts, for Sido appears not only in the book named for her but also in *My Mother's House*, *Break of Day*, some novellas and stories and in the books of reflections and memories. As the mother of "Minet-Chéri", her pet name for her youngest daughter, Sido is the loving, enabling mother figure who protects without repressing, who provides a female space from which the patriarchal world may be viewed critically, from a vantage point of safety.

The only comparable figure within the fiction is that of Louisette's mother in "The Tender Shoot", who provides her daughter, the "tender shoot", with a safe and partially enclosed garden in which to grow, and helps her to chase away the invading, predatory male. As Mari McCarty points out in her article on this story, the juxtaposition of this text with "Green Sealing Wax" in the volume "The Kepi" is appropriate, for "Green Sealing Wax" begins with Sido's journey to reclaim her daughter from "a man above suspicions who had designs on my little pointed face, the plaits that whipped against my calves, and my well-made body" (*CSC*, 387), a man to whose family Minet-Chéri had been entrusted for the holidays. McCarty accurately comments that "the mission of these mothers is not the repressive condemnation of desire in young girls" but rather to "prevent them from becoming the victim in a sexual power relationship" (*CSC*, 3). The mother's function here is not to refuse the daughter's sexuality and keep her imprisoned in childhood, but to enable her to assume her sexuality freely.

The positive image of the mother depends on the daughter's achievement of the apparently contradictory goals of identification and separation. Separation alone means emotional alienation; identification alone means a failure to grow up. In Sido and in other maternal figures Colette created mothers who are themselves both emotionally identified with their child and separate, possessing an identity outside the maternal which in turn provides a model for the daughter and leaves her a margin of freedom outside the maternal gaze. Sido's identity goes well beyond the maternal and rests too on her relationship with the Captain, on her passionate attachment to the natural world and on her friendly but irreverent dealings with the local community of Saint-Sauveur.

The co-existence of maternal tenderness and independent selfhood is also a theme of several cat stories: Nonoche, in the text of that name, lovingly contemplates her sleeping kitten but is gradually drawn back, by the sights and sounds of the garden and the tomcat's song of desire, to her own feline pleasures. In *My Mother's House* Nonoche becomes part of the "chain of mutually suckling cats" which signifies, in a delightfully sensual image, the pleasure of motherhood and the mother's continuing identity as daughter.

> . . . Bijou, four times a mother in three years, from whose teats hung a chaplet of newborn offspring, was herself engaged in noisily sucking, with an overlarge tongue and a purring not unlike the roar of a log fire, the milk of the aged Nonoche, who lay inert with comfort, one paw across her eyes. (*MMH*, 61)

If the relationship to the mother is to be enabling rather than crippling then it can not depend solely on the literal presence of the mother but must be internalised and projected on to other relationships and other areas of life. This is what happens in Colette's world, where women provide each other with a support or concern that may be described as motherly, where they form alliances based on mutual trust. Despite Sido's unique status in the texts, even her relationship with Minet-Chéri is partially duplicated by her friend Adrienne with whom she once swapped suckling babies so that Adrienne with her "beautiful yellow gipsy eyes" (*Sido*, 161) once fed Minet-Chéri with her own milk. Both fiction and autobiography contain relationships of surrogate motherhood, where an older woman supports and protects a younger. The narrator's female lover in *The Tendrils of the Vine* (*Les Vrilles de la vigne*, 1908) displays "maternal anxiety"[4] and offers food, love and protection. In *The Vagabond* Renée seeks the advice and approval of her sister-in-law Margot, when love threatens her independence, and it is Margot who leaves Renée the legacy that provides her financial security in *The Captive*.

Equally pervasive are female relationships which could better be described as sisterly. From Claudine's friendship with Annie in *Claudine and Annie*, through the fond alliance of Jane and Fanny in *The Other One*, and on to "Colette"'s affectionate concern for Marco in "The Kepi", Colette's work presents women's friendship as one of life's pleasures, and as a pleasure within which the sexual and the platonic are not sharply divided but form a continuum. The sisters of *Le Toutounier* compose the most explicit image of a sisterhood that is only incidentally biological.

These female alliances contain an element of the defensive, for both solitary independence and relationships with male lovers are fraught with problems. Fanny and Jane's sense of solidarity is partially based on their shared recognition that "Two of us are not too many to be alone with Farou – to stand up to Farou" (*OO*, 154), and the alliance between Alice and Maria begins only when

Michel's jealousy threatens Alice. But women also enjoy each other's company because they share a certain female culture, born of their confinement to the domestic sphere but offering scope for the development of useful skills and for creativity. Though Renée describes marriage as a combination of the roles of "Steward, sick-nurse, children's nurse" (*V*,126), elsewhere the most conventionally female tasks of domestic management, growing and preparing food, sewing and tapestry are redeemed from their connotations of servitude and become a part of that female space that unites women.

Fanny and Jane first recognise the possibility of friendship when they observe their "similar methods of polishing brown shoes, cleaning out the bath without using an abrasive, breaking eggs into a bowl" (*OO*,41), and Alice leaves the tense, histrionic dialogues with Michel to discover with relief the warm stove and the smell of cooking in Maria's kitchen: "How cosy it is! How human it all is, so normal and pleasant!" (*Duo*, 75).

The "I" persona Colette created through her journalism and her reflective essays displays a constant interest in gardening, cookery, herbal remedies and sewing, which she shares with an implied female readership. Any qualitative distinction between the high art of writing and the mundane crafts practised by women is refused. In *The Evening Star* "Colette" uses her lecture notes "to wrap up a piece of butter, a rabbit, a pair of sausages" (*ES*,124) and compares her tapestry needle with her pen, finding them equal in value:

> Guided by the same hand, pen and needle, the habit of work and the commonsense desire to bring it to an end become friends, separate, come together again. (*ES*, 143–4)

Concerned as they are then to displace rigid definitions

of gender, to mingle or transpose the conventional attributes of male and female, Colette's texts do nonetheless establish a consistent difference between the sexes at the level of emotional needs and behaviour. This difference, both part and product of patriarchy, generates the double conflict which structures many of the narratives: the conflict between the incompatible desires of a man and a woman, and that between the woman's desire for man's "dazzling difference" (*PI*, 93) and her contradictory will to freedom. "Love, bread and butter of my pen and my life" (*ES*, 123), wrote Colette in old age. Yet the mildly disparaging term "bread and butter" is significant, for despite its thematic and narrative importance sexual love is not the ultimate focus of Colette's writing.

From the earliest texts to the final essays written from the serene immobility of her old age, Colette insists that life is also elsewhere. Claudine returns again and again to solitude in the garden of Montigny, where Sido's imperative to "Look!" at the natural world, to replace self-consciousness with a contemplative curiosity, is obeyed. Female animals have their brief seasons of peremptory desire, when they leave behind the pleasures of human company, of hunting and maternity to follow the call or scent of the most seductive male, but these are interludes in lives filled otherwise with "silence, faithfulness, impacts of soul" (*BD*, 43). If Renée rejects Max, she does so partly because he threatens that sense of unmediated contemplation of and participation in the world that she prizes:

> I refuse to see the most beautiful countries of the world microscopically reflected in the amorous mirror of your eyes. (*V*, 190)

Love represents a distraction from more vital experience, the "routine of the abyss" in *The Pure and the Impure* (83), "one of the great commonplaces of existence" in *Break of Day* (18).

Stories of love are framed within or interrupted by "blanks" (*CSC*, 355) or "lulls" (*CSC*, 559) in a woman's life, "periods empty of love" which are not to be compared to "blank pages" (*CSC*, 559) but rather to those significant gaps which "introduce space and order between the chapters of a book" (*CSC*, 559). In stories narrated by "Colette" the narrator's own awareness of the richness of life and the myopia of love is central to the narrative: the narrator of "Rainy Moon" celebrates those "blessed days, sensitive to the light of the external world, in which the relaxed and idle senses (make) chance discoveries" (*CSC*, 335) in contrast to the enclosed, obsessional existence of Delia, who represents one facet of the narrator's self.

Several "Colette" narrators observe the affairs of other female characters while engaged in their own quests and activities, and thus frame the love narratives within a wider context: the conclusion of *Chance Acquaintances* has the narrator thankfully leave behind both the tragic and the absurd love stories of her "acquaintances" and set off in the company of her cat "to blaze a trail just wide enough for my feet and for hers, a trail that would be obliterated behind us as we went" (*CA*, 78). In *Chéri*, Léa's final adaptation to a solitary life is prefigured by the pleasure she takes in repossessing her own space and time during her lover's periods of absence.

> With Chéri out of the house, Léa became herself again, very alive, cheerful and on the spot . . . . (*C*, 22)

Break of Day states explicitly a sense of priorities implicit in the fiction:

> At no time has the catastrophe of love, in all its phases and consequences, formed a part of the true intimate life of a woman. (*BD*, 62)

Indeed *Break of Day* takes this rich plurality of life outside the confines of love as its central theme, for there the narrator envisages herself emerging from "a confused heap of feminine cast-offs" (*BD*, 18), the paraphernalia of an actively heterosexual woman, to discover "that all the rest is gay and varied, and that there is plenty of it" (ibid.). This book creates a constellation of images which amplify this central idea: the male lover, juxtaposed with Sido's precious pink cactus, becomes another manifestation of life's splendid variety rather than a source of pain, like the fire in a neighbour's barn whose beauty Sido enjoys from her bedroom window, safe in the knowledge that "it was nothing but straw" and that she could do nothing to help.

The last works, *The Evening Star* and *The Blue Lantern* (*Le Fanal bleu*, 1949), also celebrate being and the pure pleasure of contemplation, to the extent that they redeem old age and impotence. The narrator's arthritis is both painful and crippling, but it is an experience on a level with other experiences so that she can spend an agreeable afternoon "idling and suffering" (*ES*, 87), and it brings her "the liberty of the imprisoned" (*ES*, 116), the ability to travel in imagination and memory on her "divan-raft" (*ES*, 94) and to discover that "the life of a virtually immobilised being is a vortex of hurry and variety" (*ES*, 141).

In *Break of Day* (published in 1928) Colette represents late middle age as a time when (hetero)sexual love ceases to occupy any significant place in female identity, and as a time when the "road back" leads to a reappropriation of maternal values and is thus a form of liberation. The "road back" represents not regression but development. The identification with Sido, which also underlies the last works, is signified by positive images of expansion and unfolding, never by images of retreat.

Let me not forget that I am the daughter of a woman

> who . . . herself never ceased to flower, untiringly, during three quarters of a century . . ." (*BD*, 6)

a woman who had "the power of conjuring up everywhere unexpected crises, burgeonings, metamorphoses and dramatic miracles" (*BD*, 24). As she writes of the renunciation of "that militant life" in *Break of Day*, or of her "decline" and suffering in *The Evening Star*, images of change, renewal and beginnings cluster in the text: *Break of Day*, as the title suggests, takes the dawn as a central motif, linking mother and daughter by their preference for the earliest part of the day, ending the narrative as day breaks:

> Dawn comes, the wind falls. From yesterday's rain, in the shade, a new perfume is born; or is it I who am once again going to discover the world and apply new senses to it? (*BD*, 141)

In the later work it is spring that arrives towards the end of the text: "Everything is new. The new, the springtime, arrive as I write" (*ES*, 129), and images of birth abound in both texts, with the birth of Colette's own daughter forming the subject of a lyrical passage in *The Evening Star*. The identification with Sido means an identification with her contemplative joy in life, an escape from the restrictive self-consciousness of love relationships, and – as the chapter on language showed – a linguistic progression towards more experimental forms.

For the mother's wisdom is one of irreverence towards established forms; it accepts neither the binary code of the either/or nor the linearity of conventional narrative. The association of opposites, the paradox that is a recurring feature of Colette's writing culminates in the linguistic identification of death with discovery and the open sea:

> Discoveries, ever more discoveries. . . . Rest assured,

> nothing is decaying, it is I who am drifting . . . The open sea, but not the wilderness. The discovery that there is no wilderness! That in itself is enough to sustain me in triumphing over my afflictions (*BL*, 6)

The schoolgirl who received only "middling marks" for an essay on autumn because "I declare myself in disagreement with those who called autumn a decline; I called it a beginning" (*LB*, 22), becomes the old woman who expresses no interest at all in the idea of a deity or an afterlife, but nonetheless celebrate's life's ending as a time of joy and renewal. The most "maternal" of the works are also the least formally conventional, for many of the later texts cross the boundaries between genres, invent new syntheses of fiction, autobiography and essay. In *Break of Day* the narrative thread, embodied in the almost-hero Vial, struggles to reassert itself in the text but is constantly abandoned for digressions which return to the figure of Sido . . .

> We were saying, then, that Vial . . .
> How beautiful the night is, once again! . . . (*BD*, 63)

and on the next page "But let us go back to Vial . . .", an expression of intent no more realised than the first.

In *The Evening Star*, the artifice of narrative is formally renounced, as the writer rejoices in the fact that her sheets of paper are now "devoid of any defining agreeable feature, of any dialogue between imaginary characters, of any arbitrary ending that kills, maims, separates" and announces "I abdicate from humbug" (*ES*, 87).

The linear is replaced by the circular, by the sphere and the spiral, those figures towards which, in her reception speech to the Belgian Royal Academy, Colette expressed her instinctive and consistent inclination. The voyage of discovery finally leads not further and further away, but back to Sido at the centre of her garden and of her compass rose (in French, more tellingly, her "Rose of the Winds"). The way forward proves to be the road back, and because this does not mean a return to the position of child, but means rather becoming the mother, there is development and not regression. The affirmation of life, the celebration of life, transcends the individual, and just as Sido's last letter ends with affirmative signs and rays and with the words "yes yes", so Colette's last completed work ends on the words "To be continued".

Paradox, which defies simple dichotomies and explodes the principle of difference, is the central figure of Colette's work. The qualities of her writing can also be phrased as a series of paradoxes: pagan, profoundly irreligious, yet celebrating the irreducible value of life and its transcendence of mortality; passionately concerned with the politics of gender and the experience of sexual love, yet defining them ultimately as irrelevant; fluently adopting established codes of language and genre yet conforming to neither. Colette's writing is founded on creative contradiction and on the paradoxical figure of the circle whose end is its beginning – within which daybreak and the evening star become one.

Notes

Abbreviations used for titles of Colette's works: (see Bibliography for details)

BD = *Break of Day*
BL = *The Blue Lantern*
C = *Chéri*
CA = *Chance Acquaintances*
Cap. = *The Captive*
CC = *Colette au cinema*
C&A = *Claudine and Annie*
CM = *Claudine Married*
CP = *Claudine in Paris*
CS = *Claudine at School*
CSC = *Collected Stories of Colette*
DF = *Dans la foule*
ES = *The Evening Star*
G = *Gigi*
HL = *Les Heures longues*
IL = *The Innocent Libertine*
JC = *Julie de Carneilhan*
JM = *Journey for Myself*
LB = *Looking Backwards*
LC = *The Last of Chéri*
M = *Mitsou*
MA = *My Apprenticeships*
MMH = *My Mother's House*
OO = *The Other One*
PI = *The Pure and the Impure*
RL = *The Retreat from Love*
RS = *Ripening Seed*

T = *Le Toutounier*
V = *The Vagabond*
VV = *Les Vrilles de la vigne*

Notes to Chapter 2

1. Annie Leclerc, *Parole de femme* (Paris: Grassett, 1974), p. 6.
2. Quoted in Antoine Prost, *L'Enseignement en France, 1800–1967* (Paris: Armand Colin, 1968), p. 269. My translation.
3. Bonnie G. Smith, *Ladies of the Leisure Class: the Bourgeoises of France in the 19th Century* (Princeton University Press, 1981), p. 177.
4. Dominique Maingeneau, *Les Livres d'école de la République 1870–1914* (discours et idéologie) (Paris: Le Sycomore, 1979), p. 71. All translations from Maingeneau mine.
5. From the *Cours de morale* by J. Payot, published in several editions in the early decades of the Third Republic. Quoted in Maingeneau, op. cit., p. 210.
6. Raoul Girardet, *Le Nationalisme français 1871–1914* (Paris: Armand Colin, 1966), pp. 77–8. My translation.
7. G. Bruno's *Le Tour de la France par deux enfants* was first published in 1877 and was part of the primary school syllabus in French schools as late as the 1930s. Written in narrative form, it recounts the journey through France of two orphaned children from the province of Lorraine, which was annexed by Germany after the defeat of 1870, using the story to teach the history and geography of France and at the same time to preach moral and patriotic values.
8. Maingeneau, *Les Livres d'école*, pp. 100–1.
9. From *Claudine in Paris*. Quoted by Michelle Sarde in *Colette, Free and Fettered* trans. Richard Miller (London: Michael Joseph, 1978), pp. 77–8.
10. Maingeneau, *Les Livres d'école*, pp. 90–1.
11. Ibid., p. 111.
12. *Colette/Sido: Lettres* (Paris: Editions des femmes, 1984), p. 56. Letter dated 6 November 1906.

Notes to Chapter 3

1. Jean Pierrot, *The Decadent Imagination 1880–1900*, trans. Derek Coltman (University of Chicago Press, 1981), p. 134.
2. Colette, *Oeuvres I* (Paris: Gallimard, 1984), p. lxxiii.

3. The *Claudine* novels have been translated into English and published by Secker & Warburg, but are not currently available in paperback editions. References here are to the collected works of Colette, *Oeuvres I*, and the translations are my own.

Notes to Chapter 4

1. Colette, *Oeuvres II* (Paris: Gallimard, 1986), p. 1352.
2. Ibid., p. 487.
3. Ibid., p. 501.
4. Ibid., p. 608.
5. Ibid., p. 617.
6. Colette, *Belles Saisons* (Paris: Flammarion, 1985), p. 179.
7. Published under the title *Leur beau physique* or *Their Good Looks*, and collected in *Mes Cahiers* (*My Notebooks*) in the volume *Belles Saisons* (op. cit.).
8. Colette worked in film in several capacities, writing sub-titles, scenarios and being involved in the film adaptations of several of her novels. The best source of information on Colette and film is *Colette au cinema* by Alain and Odette Virmaux (Paris: Flammarion, 1975).
9. *Oeuvres II*, p. 942.
10. *La Jumelle noire (The Black Opera-Glasses)*, originally published in 1934. References here to *Oeuvres Complètes* (Paris: Editions le Fleuron, 1948–50), vol. X, p. 168.
11. Ibid., p. 125.
12. Interview with Madeleine Chapsal in Serge Julienne-Caffie, *Simone de Beauvoir* (Paris: Gallimard, 1966), p. 212.
13. Anne A. Ketchum, *Colette ou la naissance du jour: étude d'un malentendu* (Paris: Minard, 1968), p. 23.
14. Maite Albistur and Daniel Armogathe, *Histoire du feminisme français*, tome II (Paris: Editions des femmes, 1977), p. 584.
15. 'Les Conquêtes du Feminisme" in *Le Figaro*, 16 March 1924.
16. *Le Progrès Civique*, no. 303, 30 May 1925.
17. Yves Trotignon, *La France au XXe siècle* (Paris: Bordas, 1968), vol. 2, p. 108.

Notes to Chapter 5

1. Julien Benda, *Belphégor* (Paris: Émile-Paul Frères, 1947), p. 114.
2. Gustave Lanson, *Histoire de la littérature française* (Paris: Hachette, 1951), p. 1235.
3. Jean Larnac, *Colette, sa vie, son oeuvre* (Paris: Kra, 1927), p. 200.
4. Colette, *Notes de tournées* (Tour Notes) in *Oeuvres II* (Paris: Gallimard, 1986), p. 213.
5. Colette, *Belles Saisons* (Paris: Flammarion, 1985), p. 196.
6. Annie Leclerc, *French Connections* (ed.) Claire Duchen (London: Hutchinson, 1987), p. 60.

Notes to Chapter 6

1. Dale Spender, *Man-Made Language* (London: Routledge & Kegan Paul, 1980).
2. From Julia Kristeva's *Revolution in Poetic Language* in Toril Moi, *The Kristeva Reader* (Oxford: Blackwell, 1986), p. 97.
3. Terry Eagleton, *Literary Theory: an Introduction* in Mary Eagleton (ed.) *Feminist Literary Theory* (Oxford: Blackwell, 1986), p. 215.
4. Annie Leclerc, *Parole de femme* (Paris: Grasset, 1974).
5. Hélène Cixous, "The Laugh of the Medusa" in Mary Eagleton, op. cit., p. 227.
6. Toril Moi, *Sexual/Textual Politics* (London: Methuen, 1985).
7. Terry Eagleton, op. cit., pp. 214–15.
8. For an analysis of *Gigi* as a story about linguistic repression see Susan D. Cohen, "An Onomastic Double Bind: Colette's *Gigi* and the Politics of Naming" (*PMLA*, October 1985).
9. Jacob Stockinger, "The Test of Love and Nature: Colette and Lesbians" in E. M. Eisinger and M. W. McCarty, *Colette: The Woman, The Writer* (Pennsylvania State University Press, 1981), p. 85.
10. Gustave Lanson, *Histoire de la littérature française* (Paris: Hachette, 1951), p. 1235.
11. Suzanne Relyea, "Polymorphic Perversity: Colette's Illusory 'Real'" in Eisinger and McCarty, op. cit., p. 154.
12. André Joubert, *Colette et Chéri* (Paris: Nizet, 1972), p. 165.
13. For example, see the article by I. T. Olken, "Aspects of Imagery in Colette: Color and Light" (*PMLA*, LXXVII, March 1962), pp. 140–8.
14. The Surrealist poets, writing in France in the 1920s and 30s, took as one of their central techniques the creation of images based on incongruity rather than similarity e.g. Paul Éluard's "The world is blue as an orange".
15. Colette, in *Notes de tournées* (Tour Notes), *Oeuvres II*, p. 203.
16. Nicole Ward-Jouve, *Colette* (Brighton: Harvester, 1987), p. 140.

Notes to Chapter 7

1. Colette, *Dans la foule* in *Oeuvres II* (Paris: Gallimard, 1986), p. 608.
2. Colette, *Autres Bêtes* in *Oeuvres II*, p. 177.
3. Mari McCarty, "Possessing Female Space: The Tender Shoot" in *Women's Studies*, vol. 8 (1981) no. 3, p. 373.
4. Colette, *Les Vrilles de la vigne* in *Oeuvres I* (Paris: Gallimard, Bibliothèque de la Pléaide, 1984), p. 972.

Bibliography

Primary Works

A complete bibliography of Colette's published work is beyond the scope of this volume, and may be found in Michelle Sarde's *Colette, Free and Fettered* (see below). Here my aim is to provide a complete list of those texts referred to in my study: these are listed in order of original publication, with the titles in English first where references are to the English edition, and in French first where the translations are my own. Wherever possible, references are to English translations in paperback editions.

Claudine à l'école [1900] (*Claudine at School*), in *Oeuvres I* (Paris: Gallimard, Bibliothèque de la Pléaidé, 1984).

Claudine à Paris [1901] (*Claudine in Paris*), in *Oeuvres I*, as above.

Claudine en ménage [1902] (*Claudine Married*), in *Oeuvres I*, as above.

Claudine s'en va [1903] (*Claudine and Annie*), in *Oeuvres I*, as above.

La Retraite sentimentale [1907] (*The Retreat from Love*), in *Oeuvres I*, as above.

Les Vrilles de la vigne [1908] (*The Tendrils of the Vine*), in *Oeuvres I*, as above.

The Innocent Libertine [1909] (*L'Ingénue libertine*) (London: Penguin, 1972).

The Vagabond [1910] (*La Vagabonde*), (London: Penguin, 1960).

"L'Enfant de Bastienne" [1912] ("Bastienne's Child"), in *The Collected Stories of Colette* (ed.) Robert Phelps (London: Penguin, 1985), henceforth referred to as *CSC*.

L'Envers du music-hall [1913] (*Music-hall Sidelights*), in *Oeuvres II* (Paris: Gallimard, Bibliothèque de la Pléaide, 1986).

The Captive [1913] (*L'Entrave*) (London: Penguin, 1970).

La Paix chez les bêtes [1916] and *Autres Bêtes* [1916] (*Creatures Great and Small*), in *Oeuvres II*, as above.

Les Heures longues [1917] (*The Long Hours*), in *Oeuvres II*, as above.

Dans la foule [1918] (*In the Crowd*), in *Oeuvres II*, as above.

Mitsou ou comment l'esprit vient aux filles [1918] (*Mitsou*), in *Oeuvres II*, as above.

Chéri and *The Last of Chéri* [1920 & 1926] (London: Penguin, 1954).

My Mother's House and *Sido* [1922 & 1929] (*La Maison de Claudine* and *Sido*) (London: Penguin, 1966).

Journey for Myself: Selfish Memories [1922] (*Le Voyage egoiste*) (London: Peter Owen, 1971).

Ripening Seed [1923] (*Le Blé en herbe*) (London: Penguin, 1959).

"The Hidden Woman" [1924] ("La Femme cachée"), in *The Collected Stories of Colette* (ed.) Robert Phelps (London: Penguin, 1985), henceforth referred to as *CSC*.
Aventures quotidiennes [1924] (*Everyday Adventures*), selections in *Journey for Myself: Selfish Memories*, above.
Break of Day [1928] (*La Naissance du jour*) (London: The Women's Press, 1979).
The Other One [1929] (*La Seconde*) (London: Penguin, 1972).
The Pure and the Impure [1932 under the title *Ces Plaisirs*, changed in 1941 to *Le Pur et l'impur*] (London: Penguin, 1971).
The Cat [1933] (*La Chatte*), in *Gigi* and *The Cat* (London: Penguin, 1958).
Duo and *Le Toutounier* [1934 & 1939] (London: The Women's Press, 1979).
La Jumelle noire [1934–38] (*The Black Opera-Glasses*: volume of theatre criticism) in *Oeuvres Complètes*, vol. x (Paris: Editions le Fleuron, 1948–50).
Mes Apprentissages [1936] (*My Apprenticeships*) (Paris: Frenczi et fils, 1936).
"Bella Vista" [1937] in *CSC*, see above.
"Gribiche" [1937] in *CSC*, see above.
Chance Acquaintances [1940] (*Chambre d'hotel*) (London: Penguin, 1957).
Looking Backwards [1941] (*Journal à rebours*) (London: The Women's Press, 1987).
Julie de Carneilhan [1941] (London: Penguin, 1957).
Mes cahiers (Paris: Aux Armes de France, 1941).
"Le Képi" [1943], in *CSC*, see above.
"Green Sealing Wax" [1943] ("La Cire verte") in *CSC*, see above.
"The Tender Shoot" [1943] ("The Tendron") in *CSC*, see above.
Gigi [1944] in *Gigi* and *The Cat* (London: Penguin, 1958).
"The Sick Child" [1944] ("L'Enfant malade") in *CSC*, see above.
Belles Saisons [1945] (Paris: Flammarion, 1945).
The Evening Star [1946] (*L'Etoile vesper*) (London: The Women's Press, 1987).
The Blue Lantern [1949] (*Le Fanal bleu*) (London: Secker & Warburg, 1963).

The following editions of texts by Colette were also particularly useful in this study:

Colette: au cinema edited by Alain and Odette Virmaux (Paris: Flammarion, 1975).
Colette/Sido: Lettres (Paris: Editions des femmes, 1984).

Works by other women writers

Lucie Delarue-Mardrus (1874–1945), *Marie Fille-Mère* (Paris: Fasquelle, 1908).

Lucie Delarue-Mardrus, *Le Roman de six petites filles* (Paris: Fasquelle, 1909).
Gyp (1849–1932), *Le Mariage de Chiffon* (Paris: Calmann-Levy, 1894).
Rachilde (1860–1953), *Monsieur Venus* (Paris: Flammarion, 1888).
Rachilde, *La Jongleuse* first published 1900 (Paris: Editions des femmes, 1982).
Marcelle Tinayre (1871–1948), *Hellé* (Paris: Nelson/Calmann Levy, 1898).
Marcelle Tinayre, *La Rebelle* (Paris: Calmann Levy, 1905).
Marcelle Tinayre, *Avant l'amour* (Paris: Calmann Levy, 1908).

Secondary Sources

Social and cultural history

Maite Albistur and Daniel Armogathe, *Histoire du Feminisme Français*, tome II (Paris: Editions des femmes, 1977).
Shari Benstock, *Women of the Left Bank, Paris, 1900–1940* (London: Virago, 1987).
P. Chevallier and B. Grosperrin, *L'Enseignement français de la revolution à nos jours*, II (Paris/La Haye: Mouton, 1971).
Maurice Crubellier, *Histoire culturelle de la France* (Paris: Armand Colin, 1974).
Robert Gildea, *Education in Provincial France 1800–1914* (Oxford: Clarendon Press, 1983).
Raoul Girardet, *Le Nationalisme français 1871–1914* (Paris: Armand Colin, 1966).
Dominique Maingeneau, *Les Livres d'école de la République 1870–1914 (discours et idéologie)* (Paris: Le Sycomore, 1979).
Jean-Marie Mayeur and Madeleine Reberioux, *The Third Republic from its Origins to the Great War, 1871–1914* (Cambridge: Cambridge University Press, 1984).
James McMillan, *Housewife or Harlot. The Place of Women in French Society, 1870–1940* (Brighton: Harvester, 1981).
Jean Pierrot, *The Decadent Imagination 1880–1900*, trans. Derek Coltman (University of Chicago Press, 1981).
Antoine Prost, *L'Enseignement en France, 1800–1967* (Paris: Armand Colin, 1968).
Roger Shattuck, *The Banquet Years. The Origins of the Avant-Garde in France 1885 to World War I* (Revised Edition. USA: Vintage, 1968).
Bonnie G. Smith, *Ladies of the Leisure Class. The Bourgeoises of France in the 19th Century* (Princeton University Press, 1981).
Evelyne Sullerot, *Histoire et sociologie du travail féminin* (Paris: Gonthier, 1968).
Yves Trotignon, *La France au XXe siècle Tome 2* (Paris: Bordas, 1968).
Theodore Zeldin, *France 1848–1945. Volume 2: Intellect, Taste, Anxiety* (Oxford: Clarendon Press, 1977).

Feminist Theory

Deborah Cameron, *Feminism and Linguistic Theory* (Macmillan, 1985).
Nancy Chodorow, *The Reproduction of Mothering: Psychoanalysis and the Sociology of Gender* (Berkeley: University of California Press, 1978).
Hélène Cixous, "The Laugh of the Medusa", *SIGNS*, Summer 1975, pp. 875–99.
Mary Eagleton (ed.) *Feminist Literary Theory* (Oxford: Blackwell, 1986).
Annie Leclerc, *Parole de femme* (Paris: Grasset, 1974). Translated extract in Claire Duchen (ed.) *French Connections* (London: Hutchinson, 1987).
Toril Moi, *Sexual/Textual Politics* (London: Methuen, 1985).
Toril Moi, *The Kristeva Reader* (Oxford: Blackwell, 1986).
Dale Spender, *Man-Made Language* (London: Routledge & Kegan Paul, 1980).

Works on Colette

Colette has been the subject of an enormous number of books and articles. Here I make no attempt to be comprehensive but select a small number of key texts, as far as possible written in or translated into English.

Marcelle Biolley-Godino, *L'Homme-Object chez Colette* (Paris: Klincksieck, 1972). A precise and illuminating study of the characterisation of men in Colette's work.
Jean Duffy, *Le Blé en herbe*. Glasgow Introductory Guides to French Literature (8). (University of Glasgow French and German Publications, 1989). An excellent analysis of a single novel by Colette.
Erica M. Eisinger and Mari Ward McCarty, *Colette: The Woman, The Writer* (Pennsylvania State University Press, 1981). An edited collection of articles on the work as a whole and on individual texts, written from a variety of feminist critical perspectives.
Elaine Marks, *Colette* (Rutgers University Press, 1960). Good general introduction and a broadly chronological approach to the works. Useful discussion of individual novels.
Yannick Resch, *Corps feminin, corps textuel* (Paris: Klincksieck, 1973). A thorough, well synthesised study of the female body in Colette's texts.
Michelle Sarde, *Colette, Free and Fettered*, trans. Richard Miller (London: Michael Joseph, 1978). The best available biography of Colette.
Joan Hinde Stewart, *Colette* (Boston: Twayne, 1983). Written from a feminist perspective and adopting a broadly chronological and thematic approach to the work.
Nicole Ward Jouve, *Colette* (Brighton: Harvester, 1987). A beautifully written feminist reading of Colette by a fellow novelist.

Women's Studies, Vol. 8,3 (1981) was devoted to Colette and contains several original and valuable articles.

Forthcoming: Margaret Callender, *Le Blé en herbe/la chatte* (Grant & Cutler, Critical Guides to French Texts series). A close, perceptive study of these two novels which also offers a useful perspective on the work as a whole and on changing critical attitudes.

Index